The Secret Of The Palamu Fort

RAZI

STORYMIRROR
Stories that reflect you

This is a work of fiction. Names, characters, businesses, places, events and incidents are either product's of the author's imagination or used in a fictitious manner. Any resemblance to actual persons, living or dead, or actual events is purely coincidental.

First Edition: June 2019
Reprint: February 2020
Printed in India

Printed at Dhote Offset Printer, Mumbai
Typeset in Garamond

ISBN: 978-93-88698-01-6

Cover Illustration: Gopi Ovn & Team StoryMirror

STORYMIRROR
Stories that reflect you

Publisher: StoryMirror Infotech Pvt. Ltd.
145, First Floor, Powai Plaza, Hiranandani Gardens, Powai, Mumbai - 400076, India

Web: https://storymirror.com
Facebook: https://facebook.com/storymirror
Twitter: https://twitter.com/story_mirror
Instagram: https://instagram.com/storymirror

To the most beautiful girl in the universe Aairah,

To the love of my life and my greatest strength Sana,

To the most loving Mom one could ever imagine Nilofer

And to Dad Firoz,

To the sweetest sister Homa,

And to the best friends and brothers

Faiz, Gulrez and Sharukh.

A humble tribute to a legend called

Satyajit Ray

His vision and ideas inspire me so much that sometimes I feel

I am a Horcrux he never intended to make.

PROLOGUE

History always leaves marks on the face of earth. Some are ugly, some astonishingly beautiful, and some that have been lost into oblivion.

To the east of Garhwa lies 'Palamu' or 'Palamau', one of the districts of the Indian state of Jharkhand. In the dense cold and sleepy jungles of Palamu, a casual traveller can very easily miss one of the most beautiful and ironically forgotten remains of a time long gone. But if you are willing to look just a little bit closer and give these mystical forests the attention they deserve, you will see that those tangled vines, trees that seem older than time itself and the cold hazy mist shield within their bosom since centuries a magnificent proof and the sole remaining witness of an incandescent past – 'The Palamu Fort'.

If you are one of those who has been gifted with the power of imagination, you will feel the soul of the place as you stand within the age-defying walls of this fort. You will be able to hear the voices of the people who once lived there, the sounds of moving chariots, noises of the busy bazaar within the fort, the march of the soldiers, tantivies of horses, soothing chants of prayers and the sweet laughs of the women who once graced this place.

Then, very slowly when the lustrous projection of your imagination weans off, the noises fade, the shiny chariots appear hazy, the sounds of the horses' hooves appear more and more distant, the laughs and sounds of the people dissolve into thin air, the streets and the mighty form of the fort itself appears slowly engulfed by the ever-growing jungle, as if it is reclaiming what rightfully belonged to it and you find yourself standing again in front of the weary and silent spectator of that bygone era that has now been bound in the green and brown shackles of the plant kingdom.

In the light of day, the silence of the area near the Palamu Fort is intermittently broken by the footsteps of the occasional passerby, but as the day moves towards night, even those few footsteps fade away and the ruins of the fort are covered by a blanket of eerie silence that is constantly pierced by ghostly noises and howls of the creatures of the dark. The very fort which appeared so regal and inviting in the light of day now seems to be inhabited by unnatural forces. Even those who boast of having the most fearless and strongest of hearts cannot gather the courage to set foot near the ruins of the Palamu Fort.

But tonight was different. In the blue light of the full moon, Bhola Ganjhu and Heeralal Paswan were running as fast as they could among the thick bushes in the vicinity of the Palamu Fort, not caring about the cuts and bruises the bushes were inflicting over the exposed parts of their bodies. They had to outrun the villagers who were chasing them. Each had one bag slung over his shoulder. The bags were full of cash and ornaments they had looted from a few houses in the nearby Amwa village. One of their partners in crime who was carrying a gun had been caught by the villagers and beaten to pulp; so, escape they had to. They could no longer hear the angry shouts of the villagers following them, but they did not want to stop until they were one hundred percent sure that nobody was following them.

Bhola who was running ahead suddenly stopped and Heeralal who was following close behind, almost bumped into him.

"Hey! Watch out. What are you doing? Why did you stop, you fool?" shouted Heeralal.

"Heera, we have reached the ruins of the Palamu Fort! Do you think we should enter it at this time of the night? I have heard frightening stories about the unholy spirits that kill anybody who dares to enter these ruins at night!" whispered a frightened Bhola.

"If we stop outside, the villagers will kill us instead of your ghosts. You are a superstitious fool. These are nothing but old wives' tales. We'll just hide here for the night and head for Ranchi at the crack of dawn," Heera said and pushed Bhola inside the ruins.

Both now entered the Old Fort, but Bhola had a sickening feeling in his stomach that they had done something wrong by entering these sinister ruins. Heera, too, after entering the fort was beginning to realize that the adrenaline rushing through his veins that had made him enter the fort in a show of bravado, was finally wearing off. Instead, a strange fear was slowly rising in his heart. He, too, had heard from the old village folks, the stories of the strange voices and ungratified spirits roaming in these ruins at night. The light of his torch was no longer steady — it had fallen from his pocket while jumping over a wall in the village.

"It must be broken," said Heera as he hit the torch over the palm of his other hand a few times. Although the torch was no longer functioning properly, the light of the full moon was sufficient to make out the structures around.

"There! We can hide here for the night," Heera said, pointing his torch towards a broad passageway built into the wall to their left. It was relatively free of the vines and bushes that were scattered inside the fort. They entered the passageway and sat down on the ground. Bhola felt the money and the ornaments in his bag with his hands and thought it was a good heist. He wished the night would end soon so that they could leave this godforsaken place quickly.

Suddenly, he perceived a column of white smoke that surrounded him slowly. A strange smell entered his nostrils. He wondered if it was only he who had felt this and looked at Heera. In the unsteady light of the broken torch, he saw that Heera was looking at him with fear in his eyes. The smell had grown stronger. Bhola recognized the smell. It was the smell of garlic!

"Who's there…?" Heera mustered the courage to mumble a few words in a trembling voice and pointed the dim light of his torch towards the far end of the passageway. He was positive he had heard a rustling noise. Suddenly the light of his torch went out and a cold, hollow voice whispered…

"Satyabhama…."

As this name was spoken, a chill ran down their spines. The old rusty torches fixed in the walls of the Fort's corridors burst into flames – all by themselves. The passage had become a terrifying playground of light and shadow and at the far end, they saw the most frightening view -- a human figure wearing tattered royal clothes inching towards them. His arms seemed to be on fire. He limped towards them and stretched one of his arms that was ablaze with a bluish fire. The blood froze in their veins. Bhola grabbed the arm of a stunned Heeralal and ran out of the passageway. They fell on the ground as they came out of the passageway. Their bags and torch fell on the ground as well, but they did not stop to pick them up. All they wanted to do was to escape alive from those ruins and not become the subject of another one of the ghost stories that emanated from the fort.

They ran like maniacs towards the very village of Amwa they had escaped just a little while ago. They wanted to see the crowd of villagers who had been chasing them not too long ago and wished they were still looking for the two of them. The thought of being killed by the ghostly creature they had just seen was infinitely more frightening than the prospect of being beaten up by the villagers.

Back in the fort, the fire in the old rusty torches in the passageway had died. The unholy spirit that had struck fear deep into their hearts had disappeared. The white mist and the smell of garlic had dissipated into the ancient atmosphere of the fort and the ruins once again donned the cloak of oblivion.

There are many unexplained phenomena in God's world. Perhaps, some are best left undisturbed.

Chapter 1

Neil Horo was sitting in front of the TV on a lazy Sunday morning and was surfing through various channels. To his frustration, he couldn't find anything that interested him. It was the fourth day of his summer vacation. He had decided to spend his holidays at the house of his cousin who was perhaps ten years older than him and lived at Riverdale City at Kanke. Neil lived at North Railway Colony at Ranchi with his parents. He was a student of class 11 at the Kendriya Vidyalaya, Hinoo.

Neil looked at his cousin who was stretched on the couch with his head immersed in a small grey-coloured book that he had been reading since the last evening. He wondered what the book was about and looked intently at its cover. It was '*A Brief History of Time*' written by the legendary scientist Stephen Hawking. Neil's cousin was fond of reading books. He had a small library at his home that was filled with hundreds of books. His collection included almost every subject one could think of — history, politics, science, arts, story books, detective novels and even comic books! He would always tell Neil, "No book is bad. Each and every book has something to teach you."

"Robin Dada, what's so interesting about this book that you haven't kept it down even once since last evening? What are you reading about?" Neil asked his cousin Robin Horo, whom he fondly called Robin Dada. Robin Horo was a private detective. Although he didn't like to be called 'Detective' and preferred that people address him by his name, the name had stuck – especially since his recent involvement in some mind-bending and seemingly unsolvable cases in which he had helped the Ranchi Police. The local newspapers had promptly given him the name 'Detective Horo' and this had struck a chord among the people of Ranchi. The city police had honoured him by making him 'Honorary Consultant' with the permission of the Chief Minister of Jharkhand!

"Black holes! I am reading about black holes, Neil," replied Robin and closing the book in his hands, he sat up on the couch.

"Do you know what a black hole is, Neil?" asked Robin.

"Yes, I have some idea…" Neil replied, but Robin interrupted him and said, "A black hole is a region of space that exhibits such a strong gravitational attraction that nothing, not even a particle or light can escape from inside it. The boundary of this region from which no escape is possible is called Event Horizon and it coincides with the path of the light rays that just fail to escape from these black holes. Information of any event that occurs within this boundary cannot reach an outside observer and this makes them all the more mysterious – just like a puzzle. But do you know what is the most fascinating thing about these black holes?" asked Robin.

"Well Dada…I have a feeling that you won't let me finish even if I tried to answer this, so, please enlighten me!" chuckled Neil.

Robin smiled and started again, "The most fascinating thing about these black holes is that they cause the deformation of space-time to such an extent that to a distant observer, clocks near a black hole appear to tick slower than those further away from the black hole. This effect is called Gravitational Time Dilation and some scientists believe that the science behind this, although at a very primitive stage at present, can very well hold the keys to interstellar travel. And who knows, maybe even to time travel in the future!"

"Wow Robin Dada, that's really fascinating! If I ever get hold of the technology of time travel, I would keep revisiting my summer vacations over and over again!"

Robin was about to say something when the doorbell rang. He asked Somra to answer the door. Somra Oraon was his domestic help, who had looked after him ever since Robin's parents had died when he was still a kid. Somra was around 58 years old, but he did everything from cooking to gardening and even shopping for groceries. In short, he took care of everything around the house very efficiently.

Some people are born with compassion and selfless love hardwired into their very souls. Somra was one of those rare people.

He opened the large black-coloured iron gate on their boundary wall and saw Inspector Patrick Minj standing in front of his jeep.

"Is Robin home?" asked Inspector Patrick. Somra replied in the affirmative and led Inspector Patrick to the Drawing room where Robin and Neil were seated. Inspector Patrick was the officer-in-charge of the *Harmu* Police Station. He was a middle-aged man, around 5'7" in height with a slightly hefty body. He loved wearing Aviator glasses with his uniform. He had known Robin Horo for almost three years, ever since his transfer to *Harmu* Police Station.

"Hello Inspector Patrick! Welcome, it has been a long time since we last met!" Robin said warmly. "To what do I owe the pleasure of your visit?" Robin continued.

"Haven't you read the newspaper today, Robin?" asked Inspector Patrick as he eased his bulk into a chair.

Robin asked Somra to bring tea for them and replied, "No, I haven't seen the papers. The paper boy didn't come today. Somra was about to go out to the market to bring the newspaper. What did I miss?"

"Last night, an Associate Professor of the department of History of St. Xavier's College, Dr. Anand Tigga was killed at his home. I came here to discuss this case with you."

"Oh! That's really sad. I had read his papers about the temple architecture of Orissa a few years back. What happened? Was there a burglary?" asked Robin.

"We are not sure about that. In fact, we are not sure of anything right now," said the inspector.

Robin looked at Inspector Patrick and said, "What I am not sure is why you have come to discuss this case with me? I know your capabilities and intelligence, and I am sure that you don't need my consultation in a case of murder," said Robin.

"It's not as simple as it sounds, Robin. We even know the name of the killer, but we can't arrest him!" said Inspector Patrick.

This sentence earned Robin Horo's complete attention.

"Who is he and why can't you arrest him?" Robin asked, sounding very curious now.

Inspector Patrick sensed that this case had caught Robin's interest. He now replied in a very calm voice,

"Because he was killed by a ghost."

Chapter 2

"Interesting…." said Robin.

"See! I told you it's not as simple as it sounds. A homicide committed by a wandering spirit is not the usual murder mystery I encounter in my routine police work!" said Inspector Patrick.

"But, what's more interesting for me is how did you conclude that a spirit killed him? And how do you know its name?" asked Robin.

Inspector Patrick smiled and said, "That's another story, Robin. I don't even know what to make of the bizarre statements given by the three eyewitnesses of this murder. Maybe it's better if you heard their statements directly. In normal circumstances, I would have discarded those statements right away and taken them into custody for questioning, but the reason I am even discussing this with you is because two out of the three witnesses are reputed associate professors of St. Xavier's College."

"Fair enough. Even I would like to hear what they have to say directly from them so that I can analyse their story without prejudice," said Robin.

"So where are they? When can I meet them?" he continued.

"Not so fast, Detective! Where is the tea you promised me?" said Inspector Patrick.

Robin laughed and said, "Oh yes, of course!"

Somra brought the tea for them and Inspector Patrick struck up a small conversation with Neil about his school and vacation. Neil was an ardent fan of Inspector Patrick's Aviator glasses and had asked him to bring a pair for him the last time they had met; so Inspector Patrick gave him his own glasses.

"Where is Babulalji? This time, I actually read his new book! The last time, he was furious at me that I never read his books," said Inspector Patrick.

"Patrick Dada, haven't you heard - speak of the devil and he shall appear?"

"Now that you have taken his name, he'll appear within an hour or two," replied Robin.

Inspector Patrick laughed.

He gave the address of the crime scene to Robin and requested him to be there within an hour and left after finishing his tea. The house of the deceased Professor was at *Harmu*.

After Inspector Patrick left, Robin looked at Neil and said, "Neil, this case is also like a black hole. It has a very strong mysterious attraction, but nobody knows what lies within its event horizon. We have to find the truth – it will be at a place from where even light cannot escape."

Chapter 3

Robin and Neil were getting ready to leave for *Harmu* to meet Inspector Patrick at the dead Professor's house. And so, they sat down to a quick breakfast. Somra was a great cook and he had prepared cheese omelettes and *gobhi paratha* with green *chutney* for them – one of his countless specialties. He could beat any chef of any popular restaurant at Ranchi even with his one hand tied behind his back!

They were about to finish their breakfast when they heard the familiar yet peculiar sound of the horn of a car.

"It seems the devil has appeared!" chuckled Neil.

"Yes, it appears so and that too within one hour of speaking his name!" said Robin looking at his watch.

"Now that the 'Tornado' has arrived, the killer ghost has no choice, but to surrender itself to the law!" said Somra and went to open the door.

Babulal Oraon, whom they fondly called 'Babulalji', was a Hindi poet and a close friend of Robin. He was forty-five years old and had several popular and bestseller poetry books to his credit. His pen name was '*Bawandar*' which means Tornado, when translated in English and that was what his fans called him. Although, the topics of his poems mostly included courage, bravery and fortitude, in real life, he had personality traits that were completely opposite to these!

Babulalji had always wanted to write a detective novel based on the cases solved by Robin Horo, but he hadn't been able to write one till now. Every time he was with Robin trying to help him in solving a case, he would become motivated to write a novel about it, but somehow his plans so far had failed to see the light of day because of his various other deadlines or some other engagements.

Somra opened the gate and Babulalji drove his red Maruti 800 car into the compound.

Babulalji came out of the car, wearing his trademark *khadi kurta*, blue faded jeans and white sports shoes. He greeted Somra heartily, saying, "How are you, Somra? You are getting thin, day by day! Eat properly. Is Horo Babu still asleep?"

"No, no, he is awake and about to leave for some work," said Somra while leading him to the Drawing room.

"Horo Babu! Johar! How are you? Somra told me you are leaving for somewhere. What happened? I saw Patrick Babu's jeep also when I stopped for fuel just down the Kanke Road petrol pump," said Babulalji.

"Yes, Babulalji, he came here to discuss a murder case

with Robin Dada. We are going out now for that case," replied Neil.

Babulalji pulled a chair to the dining table. He hurriedly helped himself to an appetising *gobhi paratha* and chutney.

"Horo Babu, leave Patrick Babu's case! I have just the perfect case for you that will suit your caliber!" said Babulalji with excitement.

"Does it involve a Professor and a ghost?" asked Robin.

"Wow! Horo Babu you are omniscient!" beamed Babulalji.

"No Babulalji, I am certainly not omniscient. Inspector Patrick had come to discuss the same case with me. We are going to meet him at the dead Professor's house at *Harmu.* Do you want to come along?" asked Robin.

"Yes Horo Babu, of course I want to tag along! How can I leave you alone in the hunt of a deadly ghost? What if you need my help?" said Babulalji as he poured himself a cup of steaming hot tea. Neil and Somra looked at each other and exchanged smiles.

A few minutes later, Babulalji was driving them to *Harmu* in his red Maruti 800. As usual, Robin was sitting next to him in the front seat and Neil was sitting in the back seat.

"Babulalji, this car has become old now. Why don't you sell it and buy a new one," remarked Neil as their car stopped at a red light at the traffic signal.

"Neil Babu, this car has seen my younger days when me and my friends used to scale the streets of Ranchi in it and later go to *Firayalal Chowk* to have a Softy ice-cream. It has a kind of nostalgic value for me. Besides, it still runs just fine!" replied Babulalji proudly.

"Horo Babu, do you think it was a real ghost who killed the Professor?" asked Babulalji as the signal turned green and he drove ahead.

Robin looked outside the window and said,

"Babulalji, all I know is that in terms of strangeness, sometimes truth outdoes fiction."

Chapter 4

1663 AD
Palamu, Jharkhand

Satyabhama was worried and was feeling helpless. Why wouldn't he be? He was just a 16-year-old boy. He had lost his mother and father two years ago during the Mughal attack on Palamu.

He looked at his eight-year-old sister Meera, who had slept on the floor near the small earthen stove, waiting for him to make a *roti* for her.

He had worked hard in their fields, but the yield was not good. The money he earned by selling the crops barely lasted a week. He was thinking of selling his lands so that he could sustain himself and his little sister, Meera.

Sumitra Tai, his neighbour, had given him some wheat flour with which he made four *rotis*. He remembered his mother who used to cook rotis for them and they all used to enjoy the food sitting next to the very same earthen stove. He wanted to cry, but he held back his tears for he knew that he had to be strong for his sister.

"In the reign of Raja Medini Ray, no house is without a churner and butter."

Satyabhama had heard this couplet on many occasions. He was thinking of going to the King's palace and asking him for help. Maybe, he would give him some work in his palace.

He woke up his sister and gave her two *rotis* with a slice of onion. He was about to sit next to her and eat when he sensed someone's presence outside their window. He went near the window and looked outside. Nothing could be seen in the darkness of the night outside the window, but he was sure he had seen someone.

Suddenly, someone knocked at the door. He was startled.

"Who could it be at this hour of the night?" he thought as he went to the door.

"Who is it?" he asked from inside the house.

"A traveller, my master. I am hungry and I need some food," replied a male voice from the dark outside.

Satyabhama opened the door. A tall, strongly built man with a dusky complexion and a moustache was standing outside his door. He looked exhausted. Satyabhama asked him to come inside.

He made him sit down and offered him some water. He brought his own plate for the traveller and said, "I am sorry, it's late in the night and we have eaten our food. Only two rotis are left. Will it be sufficient for you?"

"Oh yes, young master. Anything that you offer will suffice," said the traveller as he took the plate from Satyabhama's hands.

"May I ask where you are coming from?" asked Satyabhama.

The traveller started eating and replied, "I am a merchant from Gaya. I was going to the King's palace, but somehow got lost on the way. Some good people guided me to the correct path. I have been travelling since three days and I was very hungry. I am really thankful for your food."

"You don't have to thank me. You are a guest in Palamu," Satyabhama said with a smile.

"Even I am planning to go to the palace to meet the King, but I don't know whether he would meet a commoner like me. I mean he has lots of other important matters to handle and he may not have the time to meet everyone in his kingdom," Satyabhama said, continuing the conversation.

The traveller looked at him and said, "I will definitely mention your name when I meet the King."

He finished his food and left after thanking Satyabhama profusely.

Satyabhama came back inside after seeing off the traveller. He was hungry. He had given the last of his food to the traveller, but he was content that he had helped someone.

To his surprise, he saw an apple kept near the empty

plate. He picked it up and ran outside to give it to the traveller. 'He must have left it here by mistake,' he thought.

But the traveller was gone.

He ate half the apple and kept the other half for his sister and slept.

Meanwhile, the unknown traveller rode ahead on his black stallion. He was joined by four other horsemen as he left the village. They rode together like thunder under the pitch-black fabric of the night with only the light of their flaming torches to guide them. They were headed for the Palamu Fort.

As they approached a small hidden door at the back of the Fort, the guards hesitated at first, but then immediately recognized all five of them and opened the gate.

"It's the third time this week. What's going on?" one of the guards asked the other, as he closed the gate again.

The other guard helped him put the heavy chain and lock back in place and said, "Who knows what conspires within these massive walls, my friend? Just do your job."

Chapter 5

Half an hour later, Robin, Babulalji and Neil were standing in front of Professor Anand's house at *Harmu.* It was an old, white-coloured, two-storied bungalow, with a balcony in front on the first floor. A flock of crows was sitting on the roof. There was an unholy aura surrounding the house. The house, itself, was surrounded by a roughly seven feet high boundary wall with a big, black and brown-coloured iron gate on the left side of the front wall. Ten relatively new houses could be seen adjacent to Professor Anand's house on both sides.

"It does look like a *Bhoot-Bangla.* No wonder the ghost attacked here!" commented Babulalji.

Three police vehicles were parked outside the bungalow and one of them was Inspector Patrick's jeep. They entered and stepped into a small lawn inside the boundary wall with four white-coloured Victorian style metal chairs and a table placed in the center. There was a road paved with stones from the main gate to the porch.

Inspector Patrick was talking with a constable and a

photographer just outside the porch. He saw the three of them and asked them to come inside.

"Come, Robin. I was waiting for you."

They crossed an impressive wooden door and entered an even more impressive Drawing room. It was furnished with magnificent wooden furniture. There was a tall wooden bookshelf which was packed with hundreds of fine books on literature and fiction by legendary authors like William Shakespeare, Charles Dickens, Leo Tolstoy, Satyajit Ray and many others. Robin took a close look at the bookshelf. The books were meticulously arranged in alphabetical order in neat rows, with each row marked by the respective alphabet. Robin admired the collection for a few minutes.

"You want to see the crime scene first or meet one of the eyewitnesses, Robin? Professor Anand's domestic help Bheem is here in the other room," asked Inspector Patrick, pointing towards the door on the left side of the Drawing room.

"Where was the Professor killed?" asked Robin without removing his eyes from the bookshelf.

"In his study on the first floor," replied Inspector Patrick.

"I would like to meet Bheem, first. I want to have a rough idea of what happened up there," said Robin after spending another few minutes looking at the bookshelf.

Inspector Patrick led him to the room adjacent to the Drawing room.

Babulalji and Neil followed them.

Bheem was sitting on the floor in the corner of the room. He was a short person of around 35 years of age. He looked anxious and seemed shaken by what had happened. The police constable told them that he had asked Bheem to sit on the chair or lie down on the bed if he was not feeling comfortable, but he didn't want to leave the corner.

"Bheem is really terrified, Robin. He was almost disoriented when we got here. We got him examined by a doctor. His vitals are fine, but he is so afraid of the ghost that he is completely refusing to leave that corner."

Robin approached the terrified Bheem and sat in front of him on a chair and pulled another one for him to sit on.

"Bheem, do you know who I am?" asked Robin.

Bheem took a good look at Robin's face and for a moment, the fear on his face disappeared.

"I…I know you! You are Detective Horo! Horo Saheb, save me! It was a ghost! He would have killed me too!" shouted Bheem.

Robin made him sit on the chair and Babulalji offered him a glass of water.

"Just calm down, Bheem. You have to tell me everything that has happened. Do not leave even a single detail out. Only then will I be able to help you," said Robin.

Bheem drank the water and started speaking. Inspector Patrick asked Babulalji and Neil to sit down. He had heard Bheem's story before and he knew that it was going to be the strangest story they were ever going to hear in their lifetime.

"As always, Professor Anand was doing his work of reading and writing in his study last night. His friend, Professor Anil Toppo, who lives next door, was also with him. They had asked me to bring dinner in the study, itself. He was working till late night since the last few days. I went to the study at around 2:00 am to give him a glass of milk. They were discussing something, to which I didn't pay attention and kept the glass of milk on the table.

Just when I was about to leave, the lights went out. It was a power cut. It was full moon, so the moonlight was coming through the window. Professor Anand asked me to light a candle. I was looking for the candles in the dim moonlight, when suddenly a strange smell entered my nostrils. It smelled of…of garlic! A white smoke slowly filled the room. I felt a burning sensation in my eyes and immediately, a wave of nausea hit me.

And then, we saw him. Out of nowhere, a human figure appeared inside the room. It was as if he had appeared out of the smoke. I could not see him properly in the dim light of the moon, but I could make out that he was wearing clothes like some old *Raja* or *Maharaja*! His clothes were tattered and his arms were ablaze with a blueish fire!

All of us were stunned with fear. A strange feeling of doom gripped our hearts. The frightening figure limped towards us in that white mist and raised his arms towards Professor Anand.

And then in the light of his burning arms, I saw that face. I can't forget that horrifying face and those bloody eyes. His face was covered with a beard, but his eyes pierced my soul. Professor Anil and I froze with fear, but Professor Anand gathered courage and stood up from his chair and asked him who was it?" Bheem was extremely terrified by now.

"Then?" Robin asked promptly.

"A cold whisper reverberated in the air, as if it was spoken in our minds…." Bheem's eyes were wide open, but still he continued in choked voice.

"Satyabhama…my curse…will be fulfilled…."

"As soon as that name was spoken, the curtains of the window behind us burst into flames! The white smoke completely filled the room. I felt a strong burning sensation in my eyes and we all started coughing. Me and Professor Anil vomited. I heard Professor Anand saying, 'Sa... Satyabhama...? Oh my God... Is the curse real...?'

Professor Anil gave me his handkerchief to cover my nose and mouth and he himself covered his face with a towel. But it was too late. My head was spinning. We both fell to the floor. We could do nothing to help Professor Anand. Then I saw a dagger in the ghost's hand. He stabbed Professor Anand in the heart with the dagger! I tried to get up, but my mind was drifting into darkness and I lost consciousness. Me and Professor Anil were woken up by the police.

When I woke up, I saw Professor Anand's dead body lying on the floor with that dagger impaled in his chest."

Bheem completed his bizarre story and tears now rolled down his cheeks.

There was an absolute silence in the room. Neil was looking continuously at Bheem's face in amazement. Babulalji's mouth was slightly open and he looked at Bheem incredulously. Or was it with a look that reflected plain fear?

Robin looked at Inspector Patrick, but he shrugged.

Robin got up from the chair and looked outside the window. He was thinking hard.

Bheem's story seemed to be unbelievable. All eyes were on Robin now. Could even he solve this one? How could a man fight with a ghost and supernatural powers?

Babulalji pulled his chair closer to Neil's. Small drops of sweat could be seen on his forehead.

Robin was still lost in deep thoughts,

"What are we dealing with here…?" Babulalji asked.

"…A ghost…and his curse?" Robin replied mockingly.

Chapter 6

1663 AD
Palamu, Jharkhand

Satyabhama's sleep was disturbed by the neighing of horses outside his hut. Sunlight was coming through his window. He looked at the other side of his hut where his sister usually slept.

She was not there.

Satyabhama jumped out of his cot and ran outside. He was surprised to see soldiers with horses and a chariot outside his house.

"Satya Bhaiya, see – they gave me these clothes and this doll," Meera said happily.

"What's the matter, your highness?" Satyabhama asked the soldiers.

"Maharaj has summoned you to the palace. You have to come with us right away," one of the soldiers replied.

A few minutes later, Satyabhama, along with Meera was heading towards the Palamu Fort on the chariot.

Several thoughts were racing through his mind.

'Why has the King summoned me? Had the merchant mentioned my name to him? Even if he had, why did the King call me to his palace like this? Is something wrong?' He kept asking himself these questions.

Satyabhama looked at his sister. She seemed very happy. She was busy playing with her new doll. Satyabhama smiled and resolved to think positively. He left his fate in the hands of God and surrendered himself to the moment.

After travelling for half an hour, the enormous outer wall of the Palamu Fort was now visible in the distance on a hill. Strategically placed watchtowers were at all corners of the walls and numerous soldiers could be seen standing on the walkways atop the impregnable walls of the fort.

After another fifteen minutes, the chariot carrying Satyabhama and Meera reached the magnificent and fabled 'Nagpuri gate' of the fort. It was said to have been imported at great expense by Raja Medini Ray. It was heavily fortified by the presence of soldiers.

Satyabhama and Meera were taken to a large courtyard inside the fort where around forty villagers were standing in a queue and an officer was registering their names and other details. Many cows and buffaloes could be seen at the right corner of the courtyard.

Satyabhama was puzzled. He asked one of the courtiers what this was all about.

"It's your lucky day! Maharaja Medini Ray moves in disguise at night to see if his subjects are having any trouble. He wants to ensure prosperity in every single house of his kingdom. Those in need are given land, financial help and a cow or buffalo. His kind gaze must have fallen on you and that is why you are here, my friend," the courtier replied.

Just then, every officer and courtier stood upright, in complete attention. The great King was entering the courtyard surrounded by his personal royal guards. Every eye was turned towards the entrance of the courtyard to admire their beloved King who had the arms of stone and a heart made of pure gold.

Satyabhama had never seen the King, but in his heart, he knew how his King would look like.

He was not wrong.

The King was none other than the traveller who had visited his hut last night.

Satyabhama remembered his father. He used to say to him, "Respect can never be bought or forcibly asked for. It has to be earned."

Satyabhama now knew the deep meaning of those words as his heart filled with respect for his King.

Then he saw one of the King's personal guards coming towards him.

"The King has asked for you," said the guard as he led Satyabhama and his sister to the King.

The King greeted Meera with a smile and made her sit on an *aasan*. He asked Satyabhama to walk with him.

The young boy was overwhelmed by this gesture.

'What does the great King want with me?' he thought to himself.

As they walked, the King's personal guards followed them, but the King stopped them with a gesture of his hand.

"You must have figured out by now that it was me who was at your home last night," said the King.

"Yes, my lord, and I am really grateful for that," he replied.

"No Satyabhama, it was my pleasure to know that there are such good people like you in my kingdom, who help strangers and give them the last of their food even when they themselves have not had a proper meal since days," said the King.

He continued: "Just like the other villagers present here today, you will also be given a piece of land, financial help and cattle. But there is a request I want to make. It would give me great pleasure if a good person like you works for me. I want you to be a part of my personal guards after being formally trained by my finest warriors."

Raja Medini Ray removed the scabbard from his waist, with his sword inside it and held it in his hands. He looked straight into Satyabhama's eyes and asked him, "Will you pledge your sword to me?"

And that was the day Satyabhama pledged his sword and his life to the greatest of the Chero kings, Raja Medini Ray.

Chapter 7

"Now please take me to the crime scene, and then I'll talk again with Bheem," Robin said to Inspector Patrick.

"Yes, of course, Robin. Let's go to the Professor's study on the first floor," said Inspector Patrick as he led them to the level-1 of the house. Robin asked Bheem to come along.

Inspector Patrick continued, "The body has been sent to Rajendra Institute of Medical Sciences for a post mortem. I'll take you there later, but I do have pictures of the murder scene with me if you would like to see them."

Robin nodded his assent. Inspector Patrick asked the photographer to bring the pictures.

On the first floor, there were two rooms — one was small, and the other was quite large. It appeared that two rooms had been combined to make a larger room. The larger room was Professor Anand's study and it also had a bed in its far-right corner. On the left wall of the room, there was a large wooden window which opened towards the outside. The window had iron grills. Traces of the burnt curtains could still be seen on the steel rod over the window. Parts of the wall surrounding the window were also charred.

There was a large wooden table on the right side of the window along the wall with a table lamp, lots of books and stationery scattered over it. There were two wooden chairs, one in front of the table and another on the left of the table, in front of the window. Bheem told them that Professor Anand had sat on the chair in front of the table and Professor Anil had sat on the one in front of the window.

There were two large bookshelves in the room that had books mostly on History and Archaeology.

A few feet away on the table's right, almost near the adjoining wall, an outline of a human figure had been made with paint on the marble floor. That was where the body of the deceased Professor was found lying.

"You said the Professor stood up from his chair and asked for the ghost's identity. The ghost stabbed him with the dagger right here in front of his chair. Was there a struggle between the two?" Robin asked Bheem.

"No, Horo Saheb, Professor Anand could not even move with fear. He was just standing right here in front of his chair when the ghost stabbed him. I saw him fall to the floor before I lost consciousness," said Bheem.

"And yet his body was found a few feet away from here towards the front wall, and *not* towards the door. It seems that he had moved towards the front wall. Why did he do that, I wonder?" said Robin and looked towards Inspector Patrick for an answer.

The photographer had brought pictures of the dead body. Robin looked at the pictures and saw Professor Anand lying on his back with his legs towards the door. He was wearing a white or perhaps a cream-coloured *kurta-pajama* which was stained with his own blood. A dagger with a golden handle with red, yellow and green-coloured stones embedded on it was seen impaled on the left side of his chest.

His head was twisted upwards and backwards and his eyes were wide open.

'Was it because of the horror he had faced before his death? No! It seems that he is looking at something!' thought Robin.

He looked at the picture carefully and imagined the position of the dead body in the room. The Professor's eyes were fixed towards the wall opposite to the door.

'What were you looking at, Professor?' he thought to himself as he looked towards the wall.

There was a framed replica of the famous sketch, *The Vitruvian Man* by the legendary Italian polymath and painter, Leonardo da Vinci on the wall.

"The Professor was looking at this sketch just before his death," concluded Robin.

Inspector Patrick, Neil and Babulalji were surprised by this discovery. They took the picture from Robin's hand

and looked at it.

"Yes, you are right, Robin! He does seem to be looking at this frame on the wall," said Inspector Patrick.

Babulalji looked at the sketch and said excitedly, "Horo Babu, I know about this sketch! It is called *L'Uomo Vitruviano* in Italian. It was made in 1490. The notes written around this Drawing were based on the work of the ancient Roman architect, Vitruvius. But I can't see the reason why he was looking at it before his death. And moreover, Satyabhama doesn't sound like an Italian name to me! Is there a connection between the killer ghost and this sketch?"

Robin did not appear to have heard him. He was looking intently at the frame.

"Could it not be just a coincidence, Robin? Are we over-analyzing the position of his body?" asked Inspector Patrick.

Robin was still looking at the frame. There was a smile on his face now.

"Blood stains could be seen on the sides where the Professor must have touched the golden frame of the sketch!

Inspector Patrick, there are no coincidences. And Babulalji, I don't know if there is a connection between the Professor's killer and this sketch by Leonardo da Vinci."

Robin continued looking at the frame, and declared, "All I know is that Professor Anand left us a message!"

"A message? Where?" Inspector Patrick and Neil asked with surprise, almost at the same time.

Robin held the frame with both hands and carefully removed it from the wall.

Every person present in the room was now looking bewildered and wide-eyed with wonder.

Neil looked proudly at his cousin Robin.

Inspector Patrick was reminded once again of the common belief that indeed, Robin's brain was sharper than a laser.

"Horo Babu, you are a genius," exclaimed Babulalji as he sat up in his chair with a gasp.

There was a message written with blood on the wall, which was hidden by the framed sketch. It read,

"H – Golden Frogs Street."

Chapter 8

“H- Golden Frogs Street!”

“Where is this Golden Frogs Street?” asked Babulalji.

The Professor’s study had again become the center of activity with photographers taking pictures of the new evidence on the wall and the constables and forensic team documenting this new twist.

“Babulalji, the important question is why has the Professor left this cryptic message, and for whom?” said Robin. “It is quite obvious that this message was not meant for everyone. The Professor had left this message for a particular person, who he knew would be able to find this hidden message after his death,” he analyzed.

“Inspector Patrick, what would you write if you knew you were going to die and you had just enough time left to write a sentence with your blood?” asked Robin.

“I…I don’t know…maybe…I think, I would write the name of my killer,” replied the inspector.

"Exactly! That would be the reaction of most people. But the Professor didn't write the name of his killer. Why?"

"Because, supposedly, the killer was a ghost," said the inspector.

"Because the Professor didn't actually know his killer. Perhaps, he also had some other reason. He possessed some very vital information that he knew would be lost forever with his death. Some dark, deep secret that would go to the grave with him if he didn't tell it to somebody. He needed to pass it on," he said after some thought.

"But that information must be of such a secret nature that he didn't want it to fall into the wrong hands. So, he concealed it behind this frame. He was sure that the person to whom this message was targeted would be able to find it. It was meant for a person whom he knew and trusted deeply. So, we should make a list of the Professor's close associates to start with and try to find that person," said Robin.

"I am on it, Robin, and I am assigning a few constables to find out where this Golden Frogs Street is in Ranchi," said Inspector Patrick.

"Yes, that would be great, but let's assume that this Golden Frogs Street may not necessarily be in Ranchi. It could be anywhere. But we have to try and find it because God knows what infernal secret is hidden there that has led to the murder of Professor Anand," said Robin, looking at the window on the left wall of the room.

He went near the window and examined the burnt remains of the curtains on the steel rod above the window.

He touched the charred portion of the wall surrounding the window and looked outside. He could see the window of the house adjacent to the Professor's residence. There was a distance of around 12 feet between the two houses.

"That's Professor Anil's house, Robin," said Inspector Patrick.

"I see. One could easily see what is happening inside the room from that window. You said there were three eyewitnesses. Was the third one standing at that window?" Robin asked Inspector Patrick.

Inspector Patrick was surprised. He said, "Yes Robin! But how did you know?"

"Just a wild guess," replied Robin with a smile.

Babulalji whispered in Neil's ears, "Neil Babu, I am telling you, it was not a wild guess. I have a strong suspicion that Horo Babu can read minds."

"Babulalji, you and your wild theories! Robin Dada can't read minds! He just has very sharp observation powers," chuckled Neil.

Inspector Patrick continued, "The third eyewitness is Professor Enos Baa, also a colleague of Professor Anand. He was at Professor Anil's house last night when it all happened and he saw it through this window. In fact, he was the one who called the police."

"Where is he now?" asked Robin.

"I sent him home after taking down his statement. I will take you there later, Robin," said Inspector Patrick.

"Very well," said Robin and again turned towards the window.

"You said there was a strange smell inside the room before the curtains burst into flames," Robin once again quizzed Bheem.

"Yes, Horo Saheb. There was a strong smell of garlic in the room," replied Bheem.

"Horo Babu, I have heard that ghosts and vampires such as Dracula are afraid of garlic. That's why people in various old cultures used to hang garlic on their doors and windows to keep ghosts away. But what kind of a ghost is this that spreads the smell of garlic before his arrival?" asked Babulalji with great concern in his voice.

"That is exactly what we have to find out, Babulalji," Robin replied while trying to move the heavy table away from the window.

Inspector Patrick joined him and helped him to move the table. There was a small yellow-coloured tumbler on the floor behind the table along with some half-burnt scraps of paper. Robin picked them up.

"Robin, I am really feeling embarrassed now. How did I miss all this?" said Inspector Patrick with a weak smile.

"There is nothing to be embarrassed about, Inspector Patrick. Sometimes, the most obvious pieces of evidence are hidden in plain sight," replied Robin. "This tumbler is made up of yellow sandstone which is mostly found in different parts of Rajasthan, especially at Jaisalmer," Robin said, as he showed the tumbler to Bheem.

"Did it belong to Professor Anand?" he asked him.

"Yes, Horo Saheb, he had bought it last year from Jaisalmer where he had gone with other people from his college," replied Bheem.

Robin looked at the sandstone tumbler closely. It was also stained black from inside because of the soot. He put his finger inside the tumbler. There was a slight trace of reddish-coloured ash inside it. Robin pondered for a minute and then asked Inspector Patrick, "Can I keep this with me for some time?"

"Yes, of course, Robin. Whatever you want," he replied and asked the forensic team to dust the tumbler for fingerprints and instructed them to hand it over to Robin later.

Inspector Patrick was willing to fulfill every request made by Robin as it was due to his genius that the investigation which seemed to be heading nowhere a couple of hours ago, now had some very exciting possibilities ahead.

Chapter 9

"I need to use the washroom," said Robin.

"What?" asked Inspector Patrick.

"The washroom," repeated Robin.

"Oh! There are no washrooms on this floor, Horo Saheb. It's down there on the left side of the Drawing room," said Bheem.

Robin went downstairs.

When he came back, the others were having tea that had been arranged from the nearby tea stall by one of the constables. Inspector Patrick handed over a glass to Robin. He knew that Robin was a tea connoisseur. Babulalji often joked that the greater part of Robin's blood must be consisting of tea!

He took a sip and asked Bheem, "Do you remember how many visitors Professor Anand had yesterday?"

"Yes, Horo Saheb. Yesterday, Professor Anand came back from college at around 6:00 pm. He was resting in his room since then after taking tea. At around 10:30 pm, Professor Anil and Professor Enos Baa came over. Professor Enos left after an hour, but Professor Anil stayed as he was working with Professor Anand.

"Two of Professor Anand's students had also come. One Dilip Soren came at around 11:30 pm. He had brought some files for Professor Saheb. A few minutes after Dilip Soren had left, the other student, Syril Munda had come. Professor Anand was very angry with him for some reason. I didn't hear the conversation between them, but I heard Professor Anand shouting at him. It looked as if Syril was Drunk. Professor Anand didn't like him much. I have seen him scolding Syril on many occasions," said Bheem.

"Did any of the two students come inside the house?" asked Robin.

"No, Horo Saheb. None of the them came inside," replied Bheem.

"Was there anything else you noticed, Bheem? Any unusual activities inside or around the house?" asked Robin.

"No Horo Saheb. I went to my room which is adjacent to the kitchen after that. I came out only when Professor Anand asked for dinner and then later I came up again to give him a glass of milk. I didn't see anything unusual," replied Bheem.

"Where is Professor Anand's family?" asked Robin.

"He had no family, Horo Saheb. He never married. He had a brother who lives in America since 20 years. They were not on talking terms," replied Bheem.

"You said that the Professor recognized the name of the ghost 'Satyabhama' and spoke of some curse. Do you know anything about this?" asked Robin.

"Yes, Horo Saheb, it seemed he was familiar with the name and he did speak about a curse. Maybe there was a curse associated with that ghost, but I don't know anything about it. But Horo Saheb, I must tell you, Professor Anand used to study old historic artifacts. In my village, I have heard many stories that in old times people used to bind evil spirits that had tormented them, to some objects and put them away. But those objects used to become cursed and if anybody tried to touch or retrieve those objects, the unholy spirit bound in them got freed. Maybe, Professor Anand had come across some similar artifact. It is not wise to upset a sleeping evil spirit," said Bheem with a tinge of fear in his voice.

Robin looked at him but didn't say anything. He asked Inspector Patrick to come outside the room.

"I think Bheem has a valid point," whispered Babulalji to Neil as they followed Robin outside the room.

Inspector Patrick told Robin that they had been trying to contact the Professor's brother but had not succeeded till now.

"I want to talk to Professor Anil and hear his version of the story," said Robin.

"Of course, Robin. He is at home. I had asked him to stay at home today for any further questioning. I'll take you there right away. But his version of the story is pretty much the same as Bheem's," said Inspector Patrick.

A few minutes later, they were entering Professor Anil's house, which was adjacent to Professor Anand's house. The construction of both the houses was almost similar, but Professor Anil's house was relatively new.

Inspector Patrick knocked at the door and Professor Anil himself opened it. He was a forty years old man and was of medium built. He escorted them to his Drawing room. It was furnished with modern furniture with a large L-shaped sofa in the corner. He was a little confused to see Robin, Babulalji and Neil. Inspector Patrick sensed his confusion and introduced them, "Professor Anil, this is Mr. Robin Horo…."

"The famous detective! And they must be Babulalji and Neil," Professor Anil interrupted him. "And I know who they are Inspector Patrick," said Professor Anil with a smile.

"Professor Anil, the commissioner of police has appointed Robin as a consultant in this case and he is here to ask some questions," said Inspector Patrick.

"I would like to help the police in any way I can, Inspector. Professor Anand was my friend and I want his killer, whatever it was, brought to justice," said Professor Anil.

Robin asked the Professor about the events of last night and he repeated the same unbelievable story that Bheem had narrated to them earlier. There was no discrepancy between both their stories.

"Detective Horo, I am an educated, rational man. I don't believe in ghosts and demons but what I have seen last night defies every logic. I don't want to believe it, but it's a fact that I saw a ghost last night and it killed my friend in front of me," said Professor Anil.

"From what I can conclude from yours and Bheem's statements is that Professor Anand recognized the name of that ghost. He also spoke about a curse. Do you have any idea about this? How was he familiar with that name and the curse?" asked Robin.

"No Detective, I don't know anything about it. I must tell you that though Professor Anand was my friend, he was not a social person. He was an introvert. He was a genius, but didn't like to interact much with people. It is quite possible that he may have been involved in something and didn't tell me about it," replied Professor Anil.

"Professor Anil, please don't call me 'Detective'. I would prefer if you call me by my name. Can I ask what you and Professor Enos Baa were doing at Professor Anand's house, last night?" asked Robin.

"Oh! I am so sorry, Robin," said Professor Anil with a smile and continued, "We were there for some official work. We have an upcoming inspection in our department and we were discussing that. Professor Enos left for my house after around one hour because he had brought some thesis submitted by his students to me for evaluation. It was a coincidence that he thought of bringing the thesis with him and left Professor Anand's house early, otherwise maybe that ghost would have killed me too. He saw everything from the window of my study room on the first floor and called the police."

"There are no coincidences," Babulalji whispered very slowly into Neil's ears copying Robin's style. Neil struggled very hard not to laugh.

"Can I see your study if it's not inconvenient for you?" asked Robin.

"Of course, Robin. Why would it be inconvenient for me?" said Professor Anil and asked them to follow him to the first floor.

On the first floor, there was one small room and one larger study similar to Professor Anand's house. There was a wooden sofa set along the left wall of the study with red cushions and a television set in front of it on a table. The study was furnished with a large study table and a cupboard for books. Robin went near the window on the right wall of the study. Professor Anand's study was clearly visible from there. He turned around and had a look at Professor Anil's study table.

"Can you tell me about Dilip and Syril?" asked Robin.

"They are both our students, Robin. Dilip is a very bright student, but Syril is a different story. He is always in the company of Drunks, and we suspect that he is into drugs also. He is an orphan. Professor Anand tried very hard to encourage him to mend his ways and lead a good life, but it seems some people are beyond salvation," replied Professor Anil with a sigh.

"Thank you, Professor Anil. It was a pleasure talking

to you. We will take our leave now," said Robin as he shook his hand.

Professor Anil escorted them to the door.

"Oh! Professor, I was wondering if you know where Golden Frogs Street is." Robin asked Professor Anil suddenly before leaving.

An expression of uneasiness quickly crossed his face. But he replied in a confident voice, "No, Robin. I don't know what this is."

"Ok," Robin said and turned around to leave. He had that smile on his face again.

Chapter 10

Robin, Inspector Patrick, Neil and Babulalji left Professor Anil's house. Someone was watching them. He walked hurriedly towards his landline and dialled a number. He was feeling very impatient. A strange fear was rising from the pit of his stomach.

It was taking too long. Nobody was picking up the phone. Just when he was about to keep the receiver down, somebody finally answered the phone.

"Will you tell me what's happening?" the caller asked in a desperate voice.

The man on the other side asked him to calm down and said, "I will be there soon."

Chapter 11

1667 AD
Palamu, Jharkhand

"Halt!" shouted Commander Trishul Singh who was leading Maharaja Medini Ray's safari in the deep forests of Palamu. The Maharaja had planned to visit their military training facility in the forest after the safari.

"What's the matter, Trishul Singh?" asked the Maharaja who was sitting in the *howdah* atop his elephant *Gajraj*.

Gajraj was the descendent of the fabled white elephant named '*Ramchandra*' owned by the earlier Chero kings. He was said to bring good luck. King Sher Shah Suri, who was the founder of the Suri empire in the northern part of the Indian subcontinent with its capital in Sasaram in modern-day Bihar, took possession of Ramchandra from the Chero kings after defeating them in 1538 AD. But the Cheros brought the elephant back after the death of Sher Shah Suri in 1545 AD.

"Maharaj, the seeker says there is a tiger around. He

has returned with his team and has seen the old carcass of a deer nearby and fresh pug marks of the tiger. He says the tiger seems to be wounded too," replied Trishul Singh from atop his black stallion.

All of a sudden, *Gajraj* became restless.

"Yes, the tiger is around. *Gajraj* can sense it," said the Maharaja and looked around. His senses were heightened and his hands were on his sword. Everyone in the caravan became alert.

Maharaja felt the stench of death in his nostrils with the blowing wind and he knew the tiger was around them. He could feel its piercing eyes on him. The forest was unusually silent now.

Suddenly, the silence of the jungle was broken by an earsplitting roar! The Maharaja saw the enormous form of a tiger jumping on him from a small cliff towards his right. The cliff was around eighteen feet away, but the tiger was going to make it and reach the King who was sitting on the elephant.

The archers in the King's caravan turned quickly and their arrows flew in air but they knew they would miss the tiger as the king of the jungle had moved like a thunder.

Maharaja Medini Ray drew his sword but he had a feeling that it was too late. He could see the sharp claws and sword-like teeth of the tiger approaching him with incredible speed.

The King of the Jungle was going to kill the King of Palamu.

But from somewhere among the trees behind Raja Medini Ray, two arrows flew like bolts of lightning. The arrows grazed the edge of the Maharaja's sword producing sparks and pierced the throat and heart of the tiger!

The tiger fell to the ground like a dead weight.

Maharaja Medini Ray could not believe his eyes. His certain death had been averted by those two timely arrows.

He looked at the tiger and saw the two arrows impaled into its throat and heart. He knew those two arrows had been shot at the same time by one person. There were many skilled archers in his kingdom, even his commander Trishul Singh was a master archer. But who among them had this ability to shoot two arrows at the same time?

He knew only one.

'Who is he?' he thought.

The Maharaja and everyone else in his caravan turned to look at the trees from where those arrows were shot.

"Long live Satyabhama! Long live Maharaja Medini Ray!"

The silence of the forest was once again broken by those slogans which were now louder than the tiger's roar.

The Maharaja saw Satyabhama emerging from the deep forest with a bow in his strong hands. He was six feet tall with a sculpted physique that even the gods of power would envy. His long, shoulder-length hair flew over his face with the blowing wind. He was no longer the same sixteen-year-old, thin village boy who had given the last of his food to his King who had visited his hut in disguise. He was now a seasoned warrior forged in the fires of a four-year-long relentless training at the King's military training facility in the jungle.

The Maharaja felt proud of him as he would have been of his own son. Indeed, he loved Satyabhama like his own son. The fact that he had just saved his life made his place in his heart stronger than ever. He dismounted the elephant and moved towards Satyabhama, who was now kneeling with respect in front of him.

The king asked him to stand up. He hugged him and said, "Your place is here, son."

Satyabhama always knew that his King loved him and his sister like his own children. He too, loved and respected the King like he would have his own father. In his eyes, saving his life was nothing in comparison to what the King did for him and his sister who were merely two orphans in an unknown village.

The king removed a leather belt from his waist which contained four beautiful daggers with golden handles embedded with precious stones. He gave the belt to Satyabhama and said, "These daggers have been in our dynasty since centuries. The belt was given to me by my father. Now I am entrusting you with it."

Satyabhama was overwhelmed by this gesture of his King.

The forest resonated with the slogans again, "Long live Maharaja Medini Ray! Long live Satyabhama!"

Everyone in the caravan was elated, except one. Commander Trishul Singh was looking at the dead tiger. He was thinking, "Tigers don't attack like this. It is very unusual for a tiger to attack a caravan full of people with weapons in their hands. And it targeted the king specifically. It was trained to do so."

He looked at Satyabhama and found him looking back at him with questions in his eyes. Both of them knew that something was terribly wrong….

Chapter 12

"Robin, did you notice the uneasiness on Professor Anil's face when you mentioned Golden Frogs Street to him?" asked Inspector Patrick.

"Yes, I did. But it does not mean that he is involved in the murder of Professor Anand. I just think he knows something more about this case than he has told us. I think we should keep an eye on him," replied Robin.

"Yes, Robin. I am assigning a constable in this area. He will be in civil clothes and will keep us posted about any unusual activities. Although, I must tell you that Professor Anil has asked me for police protection this morning. He said he is afraid for his life after last night's incident," said Inspector Patrick.

"Very well. But right now, don't tell him about that constable in civil clothes. I don't want him to know that we are keeping an eye on him," said Robin.

"All right, Robin," said Inspector Patrick.

"Let's go to RIMS now. I need to see the Professor's

body and that dagger too," said Robin.

"Yes, of course, Robin. Sub-inspector Collin Joseph is at RIMS right now with the dagger. He is waiting for the post mortem report of Professor Anand," said Inspector Patrick.

A few minutes later, they were heading towards the Rajendra Institute of Medical Sciences at *Bariatu*. Robin was sitting in Inspector Patrick's jeep and Babulalji and Neil were following in the Maruti 800. They took a right turn at *Medical Chowk* and entered the RIMS campus, crossing the famous *Durga Temple*. There were many small shops selling fruits, juices, stationery and artifacts, besides many medical stores at the busy *Medical Chowk*.

They left their vehicles in the parking lot. The place was bustling with activity. Many ambulances and autorickshaws were parked in front of the Emergency Department and patients were being transferred to stretchers. They walked towards the block where the Department of Forensic Medicine was situated. In contrast to the Emergency Department, this was a quiet place. Only a few students wearing white aprons were seen walking the corridor. A characteristic smell of 'formalin' was present all around. Robin asked Babulalji and Neil to wait outside and went inside the building with Inspector Patrick.

After a few steps, the corridor bifurcated into left and right. They turned into the right corridor. At the far end, there were three doors. Above the first door, there was a small black-coloured wooden board which read, 'Dr. Nakul Mahto, Professor and HOD, Dept. of Forensic Medicine and Toxicology'.

"That's our destination," said Inspector Patrick as he led Robin towards the room.

As they approached the door, they saw Dr. Nakul Mahto coming out of the room with a few students. He was an old man with a formidable personality. He was in a crisp white shirt and black trousers with shining brown shoes. Inspector Patrick greeted him. Dr. Nakul gestured to the students to carry on and turned towards Inspector Patrick.

"So, Patrick you have brought the Detective with you this time!" said Dr. Nakul smiling at Robin.

"It's an honour to meet you, Sir," said Robin as he shook Dr. Nakul's hand.

"Believe me, Detective Horo, the honour is mine! It's not every day that a famous personality like you comes to meet me," said Dr. Nakul as he led them to the morgue.

"What do you think of the unbelievable story of Professor Anand's murder, Detective?" asked Dr. Nakul.

"You can call me Robin," said Robin.

"Oh yes, sure," smiled Dr. Nakul.

"So Robin, what do you think? Do you believe in ghosts?" he asked again as they walked towards the morgue.

"If you ask me my personal opinion, then I don't believe in ghosts or spirits. But I believe there are still many strange things in this world that can't be explained by our present understanding of science," replied Robin.

"Yes, one should keep one's mind open to every possibility," said Dr. Nakul as he gestured to them to enter the door of the morgue.

It was a cold room, lit by a white tubelight. There were metallic locker-like shelves on the walls which contained corpses. In the right corner of the room, a corpse was lying on a stretcher. It was covered with a white cloth.

The staff present in the room removed the white cloth to reveal the body of Professor Anand. A thick suture ran down vertically through his chest and abdomen. His head was twisted upwards and backwards, just as Robin had seen in the photograph. Robin knew it was the man's last effort to send a message to someone and to keep a secret from being lost forever.

"Robin, when I saw the body initially, I thought his twisted head was due to some struggle with his murderer, but when I examined him closely, I realized that it was not the case. He deliberately did this to himself. Maybe, he was looking at something and went into *rigor mortis* in this position," said Dr. Nakul Mahto.

Inspector Patrick and Robin looked at each other. Robin had deducted this fact just by looking at the photograph of the dead body and had brilliantly found the secret message by the Professor.

"He was killed by the dagger which ruptured his heart and damaged it badly. Internal haemorrhage led to shock and cardiac arrest. Other than this, there is nothing unusual regarding his death, Robin. The post-mortem report is being prepared by a colleague and it would be provided to the police within an hour, I guess. Now if you could excuse me, I have to take a class," declared Dr. Nakul.

Robin looked at the sutured wound over the left side of the Professor's chest.

"Yes, of course, Sir. Thank you so much for your time and help," said Robin and shook Dr. Nakul's hand again.

"You are always welcome, Robin," said Dr. Nakul as he left for his class.

Robin looked at the Professor's body for a few minutes more and then asked Inspector Patrick, "So where is the dagger?"

"Sub-inspector Collin is waiting outside the block with the dagger, Robin. Let's go outside," said Inspector Patrick.

Both of them came outside where Babulalji and Neil were waiting for them. There was a police jeep parked outside the block in which Sub-inspector Collin Joseph was sitting. He climbed out of the jeep when he saw Inspector Patrick and Robin coming out of the department. He had a transparent plastic bag in his hand. It contained the dagger.

"Horo Babu, what happened inside? Did you find more clues?" asked Babulalji, his voice full of curiosity.

"No Babulalji. No clues," said Robin with a smile.

Babulalji shook his head in disappointment.

Sub-inspector Collin handed over the dagger to Inspector Patrick and said, "Sir, We have screened the dagger for fingerprints. There aren't any."

"That was very much expected, Collin," said Inspector Patrick as he handed over the dagger to Robin.

Robin took a good look at the dagger. It was a beautiful dagger with a strong sharp blade and a stunningly carved golden handle which was embedded with red, green and yellow-coloured precious stones. He said, "It does look antique, as if it belonged to some old king. If somebody has planned this illusion, he is very thorough."

"But Horo Babu, what if it was really the ghost of some old king?" asked Babulalji.

"Even then, Babulalji, we have to find the reason why he killed the Professor and what is the secret of H-Golden Frogs Street," replied Robin.

"We are sending this dagger to the experts to see whether it is actually an antique or if it has been made to look like one," said Inspector Patrick while handing it back to Collin.

Collin drove away in his jeep with the dagger.

"I guess, we have to meet one more person today – Professor Enos Baa," said Robin.

"Yes, indeed, Robin. But Professor Enos has recorded his statement with us and has requested us to let him rest at his home today as he was not feeling well. He said he would help us in any further investigations tomorrow if required. Even I have to report the developments to the commissioner after collecting the post-mortem report. But if you want to meet him today, I can take you to him in the evening," said Inspector Patrick.

"No, it's fine. We can meet him tomorrow morning. Even I have to think about the evidence we have found today. May be, tomorrow, I will have some more questions for Professor Enos Baa," said Robin as he took his leave.

A few minutes later, Robin, Babulalji and Neil were heading back to Robin's home in the Maruti 800. Robin was lost in thought and was constantly looking at the sandstone tumbler found at Professor Anand's house. Both Neil and Babulalji knew it was no use trying to talk to Robin at this time, as he would not respond to any of their questions. So, they talked to each other.

"What do you think, Babulalji, was it a real ghost?" asked Neil.

"Neil Babu, I know Horo Babu will differ with me, but I do believe in ghosts! Besides what explanation can be given for the incident that occurred at Professor Anand's house? How can a man in old, tattered royal clothes appear out of nowhere inside a room, surrounded by white smoke? How did those curtains catch fire by themselves when the ghost spoke his name? What about his burning arms? How can a man do all these things? Even Professor Anand spoke about a curse before his death. Believe me, Neil Babu, it was a ghost! Professor Anand must have stumbled onto something that belonged to the ghost and I think that cursed object is hidden at Golden Frogs Street," replied Babulalji.

"Wow! Babulalji, you have started to think like a detective!" chuckled Neil.

"Yes, I think I have imbibed Horo Babu's qualities

and his analytical mind by sitting next to him," laughed Babulalji.

When their car neared *'Bhootnath Temple'* at *Harmu*, Robin asked Babulalji to slow down and said, "Babulalji, you drop me here at the *Bhootnath Temple*. I will return home in the evening, later. You too come home in the evening. We will discuss the case at that time."

Babulalji replied, "Horo Babu, I was thinking of staying with you for a few days till this case is solved. I think this time I will be able to write my first detective novel!"

"Yes, of course, Babulalji. You are most welcome," replied Robin.

"Thank you, Horo Babu. I'll drop Neil and will come to your home in the evening with my clothes and other utilities," replied Babulalji.

Babulalji often stayed with Robin while he was writing his poetry books or when Robin was working on a case. The room in front of Robin's was unofficially assigned to him and even when he was not staying there, he often kept his things in that room.

Neil was very happy to hear this because he enjoyed the times when the three of them stayed together at Robin's house. Not only because of the interesting cases they discussed together, but also because Somra made some of his best recipes during those times! He had spent many a happy evening savouring the delicious food that Somra made while listening to stories about Robin's fascinating cases.

Robin gave some money to Neil and said, "Buy some chicken and *paneer* on the way and give them to Somra. Ask him to make something special for us tonight." With that, he went towards the *Bhootnath Temple.*

"I wonder why he is going to *Bhootnath Temple.* Does he believe the ghost was real?" said Babulalji looking at Robin's back as he was crossing the road.

Babulalji dropped Neil and went home to get his belongings.

Neil gave Somra the ingredients for their dinner and told him about the unbelievable stories of their day.

Then, with a sigh, he turned towards his books. He thought it wise to study for a while because he knew the discussion around the case in the evening would leave him with no time to study.

He was excited for the evening because he was sure that when Robin came home, he would lift the curtain from at least some parts of this dark and intriguing secret…

Chapter 13

Babulalji reached at around 5:00 pm. He kept his belongings in the room that was exactly opposite to Robin's room. Neil's room was adjacent to Robin's.

"You know, Neil Babu one of the reasons why I have come here is of course because I want to see firsthand how he solves this case. Maybe, I can help him in some way, however small. But the most important reason why I came here is that I am scared to my core by this ghost story! I wasn't brave enough to stay alone at my house. Aren't you afraid if that ghost of Satyabhama is real? May be he was there, hovering above our heads while we were doing our investigations at Professor Anand's house! What if he sees me now as a potential threat to his motives and wants to remove me from his way? My God! My life may be in danger," said a visibly spooked Babulalji.

Neil laughed and reassured him, "Babulalji, don't worry! Satyabhama won't recognize you as a 'potential threat' to his plans. You are too smart for that, aren't you? You are 'The Tornado!!' Besides, even if he does have such a thought, Robin Dada will be here with us."

"Yes, you are right, Neil Babu. I am too smart for that!" said Babulalji with a straight face.

Neil couldn't help but smile. He said, "Let's go down, Babulalji. I will ask Somra for some tea and snacks."

Both of them went to the kitchen where Somra was busy preparing for dinner. He was marinating the chicken.

"Wow, Somra, the food smells delicious! I can't wait for dinner," said Neil.

Babualji tossed a capsicum in his hands like a ball and said laughing, "Another reason for me to come here is the heavenly food prepared by Somra."

Neil and Babulalji sat on the porch where Somra served them tea. They talked about the case and waited for Robin to come home. Babulalji then dozed off after a few minutes of animated conversation.

Robin came home at around 7:00 pm. Both Babulalji and Neil were very excited to see him. Babulalji asked, "Horo Babu what were you doing at *Bhootnath Temple* for so long? I have heard rumours that the priest of the temple is a powerful psychic. Did you find any clue about Satyabhama there?"

"No, Babulalji. Still no clues," said Robin as he handed over the sandstone tumbler to Neil. He asked Somra for a cup of tea and went up to take a bath.

He came down after a few minutes. Somra handed him a cup of steaming hot tea.

"Let's sit outside," said Robin.

It was dark outside now. Somra switched on the garden

lights and placed a wooden cot and three easy chairs in the garden. Robin sat on the cot. Neil and Babulalji took the chairs.

"Robin Dada, please tell us what do you think about this case. We are dying to hear your opinion," said Neil.

"Yes, Horo Babu, tell us something. My stomach is about to burst with the suspense!" said Babulalji.

Robin took a sip from his steaming cup of tea and said, "Babulalji I still have no explanation about the mystery of that ghost Satyabhama. This is an extremely tangled puzzle. We have to untangle it, one knot at a time. At first, we have to see the facts that we have in this case," he said.

"First, according to the eyewitnesses, Professor Anand was killed by a ghost wearing old royal clothes. Second fact, it seemed that Professor Anand was familiar with the name 'Satyabhama' and he said something about a 'curse' being true before his death," said Robin.

"It means this ghost Satyabhama has a legend of some curse associated with him and Professor Anand knew about it. These stories of deadly curses are often associated with old treasures, things of great monetary value or some old artifacts. Just as there were many legends about the curse on the treasure found in the pyramid of the Egyptian Pharaoh Tutankhamen, too. The curse said, "Whoever disturbs the last resting place of the Pharaoh, death will follow him wherever he goes," Robin explained.

"These rumours were taken seriously when many members of the British archaeologist Howard Carter's team who discovered the tomb of Tutankhamen in November 1922, died mysterious deaths within a few days of unearthing the tomb. Many scholars claim that this curse was just a rumour spread by Howard Carter himself to scare away thieves from the tomb and to protect the treasure found in Tutankhamen's pyramid. The treasure was of immense monetary and historical value," added Robin.

By then, Somra had placed the electric *tandoor* in the garden and had begun cooking the 'roasted chicken'. The appetizing aroma from the *tandoor* distracted them. Neil and Babulalji kept looking at the *tandoor*, salivating at the thought of the chicken cooking inside, even as they kept trying to listen to Robin's analysis.

He continued, "So, it seems this ghost belongs to an old king or was a member of some royal family. Professor Anand must have somehow acquired the knowledge about a treasure or a valuable artifact related to him. We need to find out about the identity of the ghost and the dynasty or time it belonged to. We have to know his side of the story. That would put our train on the right track. Otherwise, all our arrows would be flying aimlessly in the sheer darkness of ignorance."

Somra brought a plate of hot steaming roasted chicken for them. They took a piece each.

"But how do we do it? I mean how do we find out about his identity?" asked Neil.

Robin continued, "Fortunately, Professor Anand was a very intelligent man. He knew the importance of this information, and strategically left a clue for a specific person whom he believed would be able to find it. 'H - Golden Frogs Street.' Although, we don't know the exact nature of this clue, I think it must point towards the ghost's identity or that cursed treasure or artifact once we find this address. Maybe, it is hidden in that street somewhere," he said.

"It is obviously very important to find the person for whom this message was written because he knows what Professor Anand was involved with. May be Professor Anand was working with him. It is quite possible that Professor Anil knows about this address. He certainly seemed to be hiding something," Robin deducted.

Babulalji interrupted Robin, "Horo Babu, I did some research about it. Golden frog is a species of toad found in Panama. The International Union for the Conservation of Nature and Natural Resources has listed it as a critically endangered species. Panama uses it as a national symbol and they even celebrate a 'National Golden Frog day' on fourteenth of August every year. It is marked by a colourful parade in the streets. Is it possible that Professor Anand was talking about a street in Panama?"

Robin thought for a moment and said, "Your information is correct, Babulalji. The Panamanian golden frog has many legends associated with it. Their local mythology says when the toad dies, it turns to gold and brings good luck to those fortunate enough to see it. The highly toxic skin of this frog has been used for centuries by the native people of the Panamanian forests for arrow poison. The story of this golden frog is really fascinating, but it somehow does not match with the circumstances here. It seems a bit far-fetched. But we will consider it if the local possibilities are exhausted.

But one thing is certain that we must find this address soon, otherwise if that anonymous person finds the message and reaches there before us, we will be left in the dark forever."

Somra had been listening to their conversation with great interest. He served them *kadhai paneer* and *naan*. They were enjoying the delicious food.

"Horo Babu, what about the smell of garlic and the white smoke before the ghost's arrival? Now don't say he might have been a royal cook," said Babulalji laughing.

"No Babulalji, I won't go so far as to say that. But the white smoke and the smell of garlic is troubling me. It's somehow stuck in my head – as if something is wrong. Something that I am missing. Even this sandstone tumbler is troubling me. Why was it there? What was its purpose?"

"Why are you troubled with this tumbler, Dada? What about it? Maybe it just fell off the table. Maybe it was a coincidence," said Neil.

"There are no coincidences," said Babulalji deliberately with a large piece of *naan* in his mouth.

Robin smiled and said, "Very true, Babulalji. Its presence was no coincidence in my opinion."

"Dada, you said this type of sandstone is found in many parts of Rajasthan. There were many kings in Rajasthan. Is it possible this Satyabhama belonged to some dynasty of Rajasthan?" asked Neil.

"I don't think so, Neil, but then again, we can't comment on this unless we uncover the secret of 'H-Golden Frogs Street'. But what's troubling me about this tumbler is not the region where it is found," said Robin.

"Then what, Dada? It seems pretty normal to me," said Neil looking at the tumbler.

Robin turned the tumbler upside down and said, "It has a hole in its bottom."

Neil and Babulalji took a good look at the tumbler. Babulalji said in a deep voice, "Yes, indeed, Horo Babu. It does have a hole in the bottom."

Robin continued, "When we went to Professor Anil's house today, I saw exactly the same sandstone tumbler on his study table."

Neil said, "Dada, Bheem told us that Professor Anand brought this tumbler from his Rajasthan trip where he went with his colleagues. Perhaps, Professor Anil was with him on that trip and he bought this tumbler too."

"Yes, Neil, but there is a very small and probably very vital difference between the two. Professor Anil's tumbler did not have a hole in its bottom," replied Robin.

"Horo Babu, it could be just a manufacturing defect. Besides, does this hole change anything?" asked Babulalji.

Robin held the tumbler in his hands and said, "Yes, Babulalji, it changes everything."

They were so engrossed in the conversation that at first, they did not notice the smell of garlic slowly spreading in the air.

Then, all of a sudden, Babulalji jumped up from his easy chair and fell on the cot screaming, "Horo Babu…it is the smell of garlic. Satyabhama! The ghost has followed us home!"

That was the moment when Somra shouted, "Babulalji, don't panic! It's me! I am cooking 'chicken garlic' for you!"

All of them laughed. A visibly startled Babulalji laughed too and said, "I thought Satyabhama had reached us here!"

"All right, that's enough of ghost stories for today. Let's eat our food and sleep. It's late now," said Robin.

They found a new topic of discussion and began talking about Babulalji's new poetry book till they finished their meal.

They went to their respective bedrooms to get some sleep. Babulalji requested Neil to let him sleep in his room, to which he happily agreed. Somra too had his meal and wrapped up everything for the day.

Outside, the night was robbed of absolute darkness by the bright full moon. There was a sleepy silence around Robin's house except for the occasional howls and cries of stray dogs.

But the full moon was gazing towards his house as if to say, "The night has just begun…."

Chapter 14

Robin's sleep was disturbed by the ringing of his landline in the library. He looked at his table clock. It was 3:00 am.

"Who could it be at this hour of the night?" he thought and came to the library. The phone was still ringing. He picked it up.

A trembling voice came from the other side, "Is... is it Detective Horo?"

"Yes, I am Robin Horo. Who are you?" asked Robin.

The person from the other side replied in a desperate voice, "D... Detective... I made a mistake... it's me... Professor Enos Baa… I took it... I don't know what to do now. I want to meet you. Wait… somebody is here… Oh no! It's him again…! No. No... not with me… not like this… please take it back..."

There was a loud scream on the phone followed by absolute silence.

"Professor, Professor," shouted Robin, but there was no reply.

By this time, Babulalji and Neil too had rushed out of their room on hearing Robin's voice.

"What…What happened, Robin?" asked Babulalji.

"It was Professor Enos Baa. His life is in danger! We have to go now!" said Robin and immediately dialed Inspector Patrick's residence number.

A few minutes later, they were heading towards Professor Enos Baa's house situated at *Ratu road.* Inspector Patrick had given them the address of the Professor's house over the phone and he himself was reaching there in his Jeep.

"What did the Professor say, Dada? Why do you think his life is in danger?" asked Neil.

"Somebody was there in his house. I think he attacked the Professor," said Robin, sounding worried.

"Who... who was there, Horo Babu? Sa... Satyabhama?" asked Babulalji. He was almost shivering with fear.

"Maybe…yes," said Robin.

Whatever courage Babulalji was still managing to display evaporated completely by Robin's unexpected answer. He started reciting the *Hanuman Chalisa* in a shaky voice.

Neil's heart too was soaked in fear now.

Robin was not paying attention to them at all. He had

a flurry of thoughts racing through his mind. Professor Enos Baa's words were playing repeatedly in his brain. He was trying his best to analyze them.

He was praying too.

He was praying that they were not too late.

Babulalji's car and Inspector Patrick's Jeep reached the Professor's house at the same time. Both vehicles stopped violently with a loud screeching sound of brakes. Robin jumped out of the car and pushed the small gate of the boundary wall. It was open. He ran inside. Inspector Patrick, along with two constables followed him in.

"Neil Babu, I don't think I have the courage to go inside!" said Babulalji.

"Me too..." replied Neil who felt a chill run up his spine.

They came out of the car and sat inside the police Jeep with the driver.

Robin and Inspector Patrick stopped at the front door of the Professor's house. They pushed it, but it was closed from inside. Robin didn't want to wait. He knew every second mattered. He stepped back a little and rammed into the door with his right shoulder. The door gave way in a single blow and he almost fell on the floor!

A strange smell entered his nostrils. He recognized it immediately.

"Garlic...! No, no. We are too late!" thought Robin.

He saw white smoke coming out of a room in front

of them. Robin and Inspector Patrick ran towards the door, but even as they neared the door, the curtains on both sides of it burst into flames. Inspector Patrick pulled Robin back.

"My God! What's happening? What is this sorcery?" said Inspector Patrick. He sounded completely startled.

They pulled the burning curtains apart and entered the room. It was dark, but the smell of garlic grew stronger as they entered the room. Inspector Patrick found the light switch on the wall and pressed it.

What lay in front of them was something they were almost expecting to see.

Professor Enos Baa's lifeless body was lying on the floor. A dagger with a beautiful golden handle embedded with red, green and yellow-coloured precious stones was impaled on the left side of his chest.

Professor Enos Baa had become the second victim of the curse of Satyabhama.

Chapter 15

Robin stood in front of Professor Enos Baa's body. He had never felt so defeated in his life. The ghost of Satyabhama had claimed another life and he had been unable to prevent it.

He was trying to figure out what had happened. The method of killing was the same as Professor Anand's murder. He had been stabbed in the heart by a beautiful golden dagger which was an exact replica of the one that had been used to kill Professor Anand. There was smell of garlic in the room and the attendant white smoke too had been present. The curtains on the window had been burnt.

But the curtains on the door of the Professor's room had caught fire spontaneously in front of him when he was trying to enter the room, as if the ghost did not want them to enter. What kind of magic was that? Could a man have done all this?

"What if it's not a conspiracy by someone, but a real ghost?" thought Robin.

He looked at Inspector Patrick. He was busy calling the forensic team and ambulance over the phone.

Robin was thinking again, "When the Professor was talking to me over the phone, he said something about making a mistake. He said, 'I took it'. And when he saw his attacker, he said 'Please take it back'.

'What did you take, Professor? What were you trying to return to your attacker?"

He looked around the room. He saw a small wooden box lying in the corner of the room a few feet away from the Professor's outstretched right arm. It was open and there was a small piece of red silk cloth inside it.

Robin picked it up.

"It seems this box contained something which was wrapped in this red silk cloth. Was his killer after the contents of this box?" he thought.

Robin gave the box to Inspector Patrick.

Both of them searched in and around the house along with the two constables. They did not find anything unusual. The ambulance and forensic team were about to reach so both came out and stood in front of the police Jeep.

"Wh…what happened, Horo Babu?" whispered Babulalji.

Inspector Patrick replied, "The ghost of Satyabhama killed Professor Enos."

"Oh my God! You saw him? What was he like? Oh God! The ghost is real!" Babulalji shuddered.

"No, Babulalji, we did not see him, but the method of killing was the same as that of Professor Anand's — straight from the white smoke with the smell of garlic to the golden dagger. But I am still not sure it was a ghost," replied Robin.

Inspector Patrick looked at Robin and said, "Robin, you can't deny what we saw. Those curtains caught fire spontaneously when we tried to enter the room! Do you still think this is an illusion planned by someone? For me, it was a supernatural experience! You yourself said that the Professor was trying to return something to the ghost. This ghost is after something, Robin. What do you make of this empty wooden box?"

Both Babulalji and Neil were flabbergasted by this conversation. Neil said in a jittery voice, "The curtains caught fire spontaneously? You...you saw it, Dada? That means Bheem and Professor Anil were not lying. And... and what is this about this wooden box? What was inside it, Dada? What was the ghost after?"

Robin thought for a minute and said, "We can't draw any conclusions yet, Neil, but it seems that Professor Enos was in possession of something that belonged to Satyabhama. This seems to be true for Professor Anand, too. It is a theory — just a theory that this ghost is killing people who have taken or stolen something that belonged to him. I wonder if there is really a cursed treasure that belonged to Satyabhama. I don't know if it is true, but this box probably contained a part of it. Perhaps, Professor Anand was killed for the same reason."

"Your theory is correct, Horo Babu. I don't think it is some kind of illusion created by someone. This ghost is for real. I don't think we should poke our noses in this supernatural mess! How can you fight a ghost, Horo Babu?" Babulalji sounded desperate. This was his way of saving his young friend from harm.

"Calm down, Babulalji. Our investigation here is over. Let's go home," said Robin.

Robin told Inspector Patrick that he would meet him again later today and took his leave.

Dawn was breaking and the ambulance and forensic team had arrived. Inspector Patrick tried to hurry up things, because he knew that news reporters would soon come along. They can't prevent this ghost story from coming out in the open now.

Robin, Babulalji and Neil were returning home in the Maruti 800 car. The sirens of the ambulance and the police jeeps were slowly fading away. None of them talked to each other during the drive home. They knew that even Robin did not have any answers at this point of time. They were trying to figure out the meaning of these supernatural incidents in their own way, but all of them were coming to the same conclusion every time, whether they liked it or not...that both professors had been killed by a ghost.

Chapter 16

It was around 5:30 am when they finally reached home. Somra was awake and was sitting on the porch waiting for them. He heard the car's horn and opened the gate. Babulalji drove the car inside.

Somra didn't ask anything, but he seemed worried about what had happened. Neil and Babulalji told him about the murder of Professor Enos Baa by the ghost of Satyabhama.

Robin sat on the wooden cot which was still in the garden since the previous night. Babulalji and Neil sat on the easy chairs. They were feeling tired and exhausted, but none of them made any attempt to go back to bed.

They were still lost in deep thoughts.

Somra brought three cups of hot steaming tea for them. They drank their tea in silence.

After a few minutes, Babulalji felt a bit normal and began talking to Neil.

Robin stretched himself on the cot and closed his eyes. Babulalji and Neil started walking around in the garden – anything to distract themselves from the horror of the night before.

There were many beautiful flowers in Robin's garden. The flower pots were kept in a row along the boundary walls. There was a bonsai mango tree in a pot, besides a guava tree also which had a few guavas hanging from its branches.

Babulalji knew Somra was the one who took care of the garden. He appreciated the work he had done.

Babulalji came back to his chair and sat in front of Robin.

"Horo Babu, Somra really takes good care of your garden. But you know what, I think your flower pots should be rearranged," said Babulalji.

Robin replied while lying on the cot with his eyes closed, "Why Babulalji? What's wrong with the flower pots?"

Babulalji sat on the side of the cot, and said," You see, Horo Babu, the flower pots along the front wall have more flowers and the pots along the right wall of the boundary have comparatively fewer flowers. So, if you take a few flower pots from the front row and put them in the right row, and similarly take some pots from the right row and put them in the front row, they would look more evenly distributed. Don't you think so?"

Robin immediately sat up on the cot and said, "Babulalji you are a genius! What would I do without you?"

"Oh, It's nothing, Horo Babu. I have very deep knowledge of flowers. I have even written a whole poetry book on flowers. It's named *Pushp Pakheru.* You should read it sometime," said Babulalji, while still looking at the flowers.

Robin laughed and said, "Babulalji, I am not talking about the flowers! You don't know what you have done!"

Babulalji turned towards Robin. He sounded confused and said, "What have I done, Horo Babu?"

Robin laughed again and got up from the cot.

"Don't worry, Babulalji, I will tell you later. Let's take some rest now and then get dressed. We may have to go to the police station, today," said Robin and went inside.

Babulalji was still confused. "Sometimes, I feel Horo Babu has a loose screw in his brain!" he said to Neil.

Neil just smiled and shrugged.

Babulalji went inside to rest and freshen up.

So much had already happened. And the day had not even really begun.

Chapter 17

Robin was sitting beside the telephone in the Drawing room. Going through the newspaper, he was eagerly waiting for a call. There was news of Professor Anand's murder, but there was no mention of a ghost being involved in it. The Police Department had tried to conceal this information from the public for now – perhaps in a bid to explain things more logically before they reach any conclusion. They knew it would spark many unwanted rumours and mass hysteria.

Babulalji and Neil were sitting on the sofa, watching television, but their attention was on Robin. Babulalji leaned towards Neil while looking at Robin and whispered, "Neil Babu have you noticed Horo Babu seems a little bit on the edge? Even when I gave him my brilliant idea about his garden, he behaved strangely. Do you think this case has affected his mind?"

"I can hear you, Babulalji," said Robin.

Babulalji chuckled and said, "I was just kidding, Horo Babu! By the way, whose call are you expecting?"

"I am waiting for Inspector Patrick's call. He had called Syril Munda and Dilip Soren to the police station for questioning. He said he would give me a call when they come," replied Robin.

"Oh, those students of Professor Anand? Yes, Horo Babu, we should interrogate them as soon as possible. Otherwise, the speed with which Satyabhama is killing people, we will soon run out of witnesses," said a worried Babulalji.

That was the moment when the telephone rang. Robin picked it up, immediately. Inspector Patrick was on the other end. He informed Robin that Syril Munda and Dilip Soren were now present in the police station and asked him to come.

Robin kept the receiver back and said, "Let's go, Babulalji. We have to work fast now."

They were about to leave when Somra asked, "Babulalji, what do you want to eat for lunch?"

Babulalji replied, "Somra cook whatever you want, but please don't use garlic in it!"

They laughed and left for the police station.

It took them around half an hour to reach *Harmu* Police Station. They went straight to Inspector Patrick's chamber. He was sitting in his chair. Robin sat on a chair in front of the table. Babulalji and Neil sat on the sofa in the corner of the chamber.

"Robin, news reporters were there at Professor Enos' house today. They somehow knew about what had happened. Even some local people saw us entering his house in the morning. The story of the ghost is now out in the open. Apparently, nobody in my department has talked to anybody about the involvement of a ghost in the murder, but one can't be sure. Maybe someone did," said Inspector Patrick sounding confused and worried.

"It was bound to happen. We were never meant to conceal this information. The person who is doing all this wants this information leaked. He wants to spread this rumour that a ghost is on a killing spree. It somehow serves his purpose," said Robin.

"You still think it's not a ghost?" Neil, Babulalji and Inspector Patrick asked him almost at the same time.

"The majority is against me it seems! So, I won't comment on it right now. Let's get on with what we came here for," said Robin.

"Yes, of course. Both of them are here and we have recorded their statements too. Whom do you want to meet first, Robin? Syril or Dilip?" asked Inspector Patrick.

"Let's start with Dilip," said Robin.

Inspector Patrick nodded and asked a constable to send Dilip Soren in.

Dilip seemed to be a mild-mannered person with short hair and medium build. Wearing specs and a half-sleeved pink linen shirt with blue jeans, he asked for permission to come in.

Inspector Patrick asked him to enter and gestured him to sit on the chair adjacent to Robin's. He appeared uncomfortable.

Inspector Patrick handed him a glass of water and said, "Don't worry, Dilip. We just want to ask some questions."

"Yes, sure," said Dilip.

Robin turned towards Dilip and asked, "The night Professor Anand was murdered, you had met him. Is that correct?"

Dilip gulped some water and replied, "Y…Yes. I met him, but left within a few minutes. I am doing my PhD. and Professor Anand was my guide. I went there to show him some papers regarding my thesis. But he was busy. He asked me to meet him the next day in the department. I…I shouldn't ask this, but I had a talk with Anil sir. He said a ghost had killed Anand sir. Is this true? There was nothing in the newspapers about this today. I thought Anil sir was in shock."

"What more did he tell you?" asked Inspector Patrick.

"Nothing more…he just said he is frightened and has asked for police protection," replied Dilip.

"Did you notice anything unusual in or around his house?"

Dilip thought for a moment and replied, "I didn't notice anything unusual. I couldn't have even if there was something unusual. I was not paying attention, really. It was just a regular trip for me."

After a moment, he said, "Yes, one more thing. I saw Syril returning from Anand sir's house."

"You saw Syril returning from the Professor's house? Are you sure?" asked Robin.

"Yes, I did. I am sure. Why?" asked Dilip.

"Oh, it's nothing. How is this Syril? Is he your friend?" asked Robin in a casual tone.

"He is a good student. He is also doing his PhD. and his guide too was Anand sir. But he is always in bad company. He has this bad habit of excessive drinking. I sometimes feel he is into drugs too. On many occasions, he has come drunk to the college. Professor Anand always used to scold him. Even I don't talk to him much because of his bad habits and the company he keeps," replied Dilip.

"Very well, Dilip, you can go now. We will call you if we need you again," said Robin.

Dilip thanked him and rose up from his chair. Just when he was about to leave the room, Robin asked, "Dilip, do you know where 'H-Golden Frogs Street' is?".

Dilip turned back confused and said, "I don't know any street of this name. Is it here in Ranchi? But I can help you find it."

"Oh no, it's fine. I will find it," said Robin.

Dilip left the chamber.

Inspector Patrick looked at Robin and said, "I have appointed a constable to keep an eye on him, Robin. But why did you ask him about seeing Syril returning from Professor Anand's house? Bheem did tell us that both Dilip and Syril came to meet the Professor that evening."

"Yes, he did, but he said Syril came to the house after Dilip. Dilip saw him returning from the Professor's house while he was going there. That means Syril visited the Professor's house twice that evening. Once before Dilip, when Bheem did not see him and once after Dilip left the house, when Bheem did see him," reasoned Robin thinking deeply.

"Oh yes, you are right, Robin," said Inspector Patrick impressed.

"Let's have a talk with Syril now. Maybe, he will clarify the reason for his two visits that evening," replied Robin.

Inspector Patrick asked a constable to bring Syril in.

Contrary to Dilip, Syril Munda seemed confident and a bit arrogant too. He had shoulder-length hair and a beard that he did not seem to have shaved for a few days. He was wearing a black full-sleeve V-neck T shirt with blue jeans.

He sat on the chair in front of Inspector Patrick without being asked to sit down.

Robin looked at him and asked, "Syril, why did you go to Professor Anand's house on the day he was killed?"

Syril turned towards him and looked into his eyes. He said, "Yes, I went there. He had called me. He had asked me to prepare some notes, but I couldn't do them. He called me, scolded me and sent me back. His domestic help Bheem had seen me. You can ask him — I left after Professor Anand scolded me."

"Professor Anand scolded you often -- we have heard that. You must be very angry with him?" asked Robin.

"Yes, I was angry with him. But if you want to ask me whether I killed him because of my anger, then the answer is no! I don't know anything about what happened there after I left," Syril replied calmly.

"Where did you go from there, Syril?" Robin asked again.

"I went back to my hostel," he replied.

"But you went to Professor Anand's house twice that day," said Robin.

"Twice…?" he questioned.

"Yes, twice…didn't you go there before also? Before Professor Anand scolded you? Somebody saw you, Syril. So, why did you make that first visit?" asked Robin again sternly.

Syril looked at Robin. He was trying to figure out who he was. After a few seconds, he said, "I know you. You are Robin Horo, the detective! Look, Detective, if you think I have killed him, then you are wrong. I went there earlier for the same reason, because he had called me. I didn't meet him earlier and returned back from his gate because I was drunk. I went back to get some cigarettes to conceal the smell of the alcohol, but despite doing all that, he sensed that I had been drinking and shouted at me. I don't know anything more than this about that night."

"Very well, Syril. But I need your help in something. I am looking for an address. Can you help me find it?"

"An address? What address?" asked Syril.

"H-Golden Frogs Street," replied Robin.

That was the only moment when Syril seemed suddenly uncomfortable for the first time during the entire conversation. He tried very hard to hide his expressions and said, "Never heard of it. Can I go now?"

"Yes, you can go," said Robin.

Syril stormed out of the room. When he came out of the police station, he saw Dilip still standing outside.

"What are you still doing here?" he asked.

"Nothing, I was just looking for an autorickshaw," replied Dilip.

"Can I drop you somewhere?" asked Syril.

"No, no. It's fine," he replied.

"Suit yourself," said Syril and left on his motorcycle.

Back in Inspector Patrick's chamber, Babulalji was convinced that Syril was guilty somehow. He said, "Horo Babu, I am telling you, this guy Syril is certainly involved in these murders. I don't think he was telling the truth. He knows why the ghost is murdering people or maybe he himself had somehow summoned the ghost and making him kill people. What do you think?"

"He certainly seems to be hiding something, Babulalji. We are seeing just the tip of this iceberg. It goes way down. Everyone right from Professor Anil to Syril has lied to us. But I am feeling lucky today," replied Robin.

"Mark my words, Neil Babu. I have solved this case! Syril is the culprit. Did you see his eyes? He had a demonic shine in his eyes!" whispered Babulalji in Neil's ears.

"Babulalji, please! He did not have any 'demonic shine' in his eyes!" Neil laughed while replying.

"Inspector Patrick, I need your help tonight," said Robin.

"Yes, Robin, tell me. What do you want?" asked Inspector Patrick.

"I will spend the night watching Professor Anand's house from a safe distance. Maybe nothing will happen tonight, but if it does, I may need you. Neil or Babulalji will call if it comes to that. You will have to be alert tonight and reach there within a few minutes, if either of them call you," said Robin.

"Alright, Robin. I will try to reach as soon as possible if they call me. But what are you expecting to happen tonight?" asked Inspector Patrick.

"Maybe nothing or maybe, everything. Please ask your constable who is on duty there today to take leave. I don't want any policeman, not even in civil clothes near Professor Anand's house tonight," replied Robin.

"Whatever you say, Robin. By the way, Sub-inspector Collin had called today morning. The experts to whom we sent the daggers for analysis said that these are actual antique pieces. The carvings on the handle and blades correspond to the designs seen in the region of Rohtasgarh and Shergarh during Mughal rule in India. Those daggers certainly belong to some old dynasty, Robin," said Inspector Patrick.

"Very well. Let's hope we meet tonight," said Robin as he took his leave.

They left the police station and moved towards their car. Babulalji was visibly worried. He asked, "Horo Babu, why do you want to guard Professor Anand's house tonight? Everything you said just went above my head. Besides, why do you want to go to a haunted place? Even the daggers belong to an old dynasty. It means the ghost is real. Maybe he is still wandering around that house. We should not go there at night."

"Babulalji, it will be fun. We'll spend the night together in your car," said Robin.

"Horo Babu, you are going to get me killed, I am sure. Why can't we call our 'fourth musketeer' this time?" asked Babulalji with a sigh.

"We will need 'him' Babulalji, but not now," said Robin.

Suddenly, Robin stopped. He was looking at something across the street. Then he casually turned towards them and continued, "Now, I need both of you to slowly move towards the car and keep it started. You may need to follow me."

"Follow you? Why Dada? Where are you going?" asked a confused Neil.

"I am going to run towards that man in black T shirt and blue jeans right behind me across the street. We are being followed, Neil! I saw him today morning also when we were returning home from Professor Enos' house," said Robin and he ran towards that man.

The man saw Robin coming towards him and immediately tried to flee. He hurried towards a narrow road behind the street pushing people out of his way. Robin followed him with the speed of a bullet! The man kicked a heap of plastic utensils and buckets on the road displayed outside a roadside shop to create hurdles in the path for Robin, but with a swift somersault, Robin catapulted over a car parked on the side of the narrow road and jumped ahead. He was not willing to let his quarry go.

Meanwhile, Neil had informed Inspector Patrick and he followed them in his Jeep with Neil and Babulalji. It was not possible to enter the narrow road so he drove his vehicle towards the other end of the road.

The distance between the man and Robin was rapidly decreasing. He was no match for Robin's speed and agility. The distance between them was now just a few feet when Robin stretched his right arm and got a grip on the man's wrist! He saw a tattoo of a hawk on his wrist.

Just then, the narrow road ended and they were out on the main road. A black Chevrolet hit Robin and he was thrown a few feet away on the road! The man he was following turned back and quickly sat in the black Chevrolet. The car now turned towards the other side of the road through an opening in the divider and sped away. It was not possible for Robin to get up and follow the car. He tried to have a look at the number plate, but it was covered.

Inspector Patrick's jeep entered the road just then and he climbed out and ran towards Robin. Neil and Babulalji followed him.

"Are you okay? Who was that man?" asked Inspector Patrick as he helped Robin to get up.

"Yes, I am fine. No serious injuries. I was just about to catch him when the car hit me. The number plate of the car was also covered," said Robin, sounding very disappointed.

Inspector Patrick informed his station over the wireless to spread the information to all stations and traffic police to look out for a black Chevrolet.

"There was a tattoo of a 'hawk' on his wrist. Do you have any record of a criminal with a similar tattoo at your police station?" asked Robin.

"Yes, I do recall that sometime ago, when I had joined the *Harmu* Police Station, I had investigated two different cases of murder and in both of them, the suspects had a hawk tattooed on their wrists. The cases could not be concluded as both the suspects died unnatural deaths and the trail went cold."

Then, he turned to Robin and said, "Robin, do we need to take you to a hospital?"

"No, I am perfectly fine. We will just head home," said Robin.

Inspector Patrick dropped them near Babulalji's car and they headed home.

"Babulalji, we will leave for Professor Anand's house at around 7:30 pm. The police constable who is on duty there would leave around that time," said Robin.

"Alright, Horo Babu. By the way, did you notice Syril was also wearing a black T shirt and jeans today just like the man who was following us? I bet he too has a Hawk tattoo on his wrist!" said Babulalji.

"Yes, Babulalji, you are right. He was wearing a full-sleeves T shirt so we can't be sure whether he had the tattoo or not under his sleeves," replied Robin.

Just as they neared the *Bhootnath Temple*, Robin asked them to drop him there and to be prepared for the night.

"Neil Babu, I don't understand what Robin is doing at the *Bhootnath Temple*?" said Babulalji as he watched Robin crossing the road.

Neil said, "It is impossible to guess what's going on in his mind, Babulalji. So let's do what he has asked us to do. The night is going to be long."

Chapter 18

It was around 8:00 pm when Robin, Babulalji and Neil reached Professor Anand's house. They parked their car some meters away from his house besides a tree on the side of the road. The place was comparatively darker, but the Professor's house was clearly visible from there.

Babulalji had packed lots of biscuits and water with him in the car. He had declared that he gets hungry when he stays awake at night.

Babulalji was in the driver's seat. Robin was sitting next to him and Neil was in the back seat as usual. Neil asked, "Dada, you are killing us with suspense. Whom are we waiting for? What's going to happen?"

Babulalji asked too, "Yes, Horo Babu, my heart is running like a stallion in my chest! Please tell us something."

Robin replied, while keeping his gaze fixed at the Professor's house, "Have some patience, please. Just watch the activities around the house carefully."

"Horo Babu, please tell me you are not expecting Satyabhama to come here tonight, are you?" asked Babulalji.

"Maybe," replied Robin.

"I don't think I will be able to complete my next poetry book. Horo Babu will definitely get me killed this time!" replied a nervous Babulalji.

After sitting for two hours in the car, Babulalji and Neil ate some biscuits and drank some water. It was getting extremely boring for them now.

Neil stretched himself on the backseat and Babulalji adjusted his seat a little back to be more comfortable. After 10:00 pm, the activities in the area had markedly decreased. Only a few occasional pedestrians and vehicles passed by.

Babulalji asked Robin to rest a little, but he declined. Babulalji and Neil had occasional conversations, but gradually, they dozed off.

The night was progressing at a lethargic pace, indifferent to whatever was happening under its dark blanket.

Neil suddenly woke up, startled by Robin's voice.

"Neil…Neil…wake up!" Robin was saying urgently.

"Wh…What happened, Dada?" he asked and hurriedly sat up on the backseat. He saw Babulalji was also awake and was rubbing his eyes.

"Don't make any sound and look," said Robin, pointing his fingers towards Professor Anand's house.

Babulalji and Neil looked towards the house. Initially, they could not see anything in the darkness, but when they strained their eyes, they saw a black human shadow moving towards the Professor's house.

"Oh my God! Who is he, Horo Babu?" whispered Babulalji. He was visibly frightened.

Neil's heart was also racing in his chest. He could feel his own heartbeat. He looked at his wristwatch. It was 3:00 am.

Meanwhile, the dark shadow had reached the Professor's house. He looked around to make sure that nobody was watching, then he quickly jumped up and held on to the upper part of the boundary wall. He pushed himself up and climbed the wall. He again looked around to see if the coast was clear and jumped inside Professor Anand's house.

Neil and Babulalji were watching wide-eyed.

In that very moment when the shadow jumped up the boundary, Robin climbed out of the car and asked Babulalji to call Inspector Patrick.

Robin waited for five minutes and then ran towards the house. He reached the boundary wall and with a single swift jump, he was on the top of the wall and in another second, on the other side!

Babulalji was amazed by his speed and swiftness!

"Neil Babu that wall is seven feet high! How did he…?" Babulalji was dumbstruck sitting with the phone in his hand.

"Babulalji! Call inspector Patrick! Hurry up!" Neil cautioned.

Babulalji called Inspector Patrick at once. The Inspector said he would be on his way within a moment.

Neil and Babulalji waited inside the car. Robin had told them to wait for Inspector Patrick and enter the house only with the Inspector.

But the wait was killing them. There was a storm of thoughts in their heads and their hearts were racing like a bullet train. They were scared even to blink their eyes. They were constantly looking at the Professor's house thinking about the man who had entered the house at this hour of the night. How had Robin known that he would be here tonight? What was happening inside the house? Would the killer be caught tonight?

They could do nothing but wait….

Chapter 19

Inside Professor Anand's house, the mysterious intruder was searching for something in the Drawing room in the dim light of a pencil torch. It appeared that he knew where the object he was searching for was placed. He went straight to the large bookshelf in the Drawing room.

Robin had followed the mysterious shadow and had entered the Drawing room without making a sound in the dark. Everything was untouched and had been left the way it was when he had last come to the house. Bheem was now living at Professor Anil's house as the police had sealed Professor Anand's house. Robin stood at a safe distance from the intruder so that he could not sense his presence in the room.

The books in the shelf were arranged meticulously in alphabetical order. The intruder pointed the beam of his pencil torch to the row containing book titles beginning with 'T'.

The object he was looking for was not in row 'T' of the bookshelf. He was confused.

'It should have been here, ' he said to himself.

He looked again, but it was clearly not there. He decided to search the whole shelf for it, but before he could begin, a voice resonated in the room, "You should look in the row 'G'."

Robin had decided to intervene.

The mysterious intruder quickly turned around in surprise. Robin could not see his face as he was wearing a hood. Besides, there was complete darkness in the Drawing room.

Suddenly, the intruder lunged across and attacked Robin. That was the mistake he made, because he didn't know that the person he was going to attack was an expert in mixed martial arts. Robin blocked a blow by the intruder's right hand with his left arm and like a bolt of lightning planted a devastating punch on his chest with his right hand! The intruder was thrown across the room hitting the wall of the opposite side. It felt as if he had been hit by an iron hammer!

Robin quickly switched on the lights of the Drawing room and the mysterious shadow was now bathed in white light.

He was none other than….

"…Syril Munda!" exclaimed Robin.

"I knew someone would be here tonight and you proved me right, Syril," he continued as he pointed his licensed pistol towards him. "I would ask you to remove all firearms you are carrying." said Robin.

"I am not armed, Detective. I am not a criminal," replied Syril.

Just at that moment, Inspector Patrick, Babulalji and Neil barged into the house. When Babulalji had called Inspector Patrick, he was in the police station itself and it had taken him only five minutes to reach there. They entered the Drawing room and were surprised out of their wits by the scene in front of them.

Robin was standing in the room with his pistol pointed towards Syril who was lying on the floor.

Babulalji was elated.

"I told you Horo Babu! Syril is the culprit! See for yourself!" he shouted.

Inspector Patrick asked, "What's this, Robin? Why has Syril come here stealthily in the middle of the night like a thief? Is he involved in the murder of Professor Anand?"

The constables who had come with Inspector Patrick searched Syril Munda for any firearms. He was carrying none.

Robin kept his pistol back in his pocket and said, "I don't know whether he is involved in the Professor's murder, but what I know is that right now, Syril has come to the address which we have been looking for since the past two days. H-Golden Frogs Street!"

"H-Golden Frogs Street?" Inspector Patrick, Babulalji and Neil exclaimed in unison.

"Yes, Syril has come to the H-Golden Frogs Street," said Robin in a calm voice.

"But…But Horo Babu, where is the Golden Frogs Street? What are you talking about? The road outside the house is '*Harmu* Road'. How could it be the Golden Frogs Street?" Babulalji was now extremely confused and restless.

"Because Babulalji, 'H-Golden Frogs Street' is not the name of any street! Neither is it an address," replied Robin.

"H-Golden Frogs Street is not the name of a street? Then what is it, Robin?" asked Inspector Patrick.

Neil and Babulalji were looking at Robin, open-mouthed.

Robin continued, "H-Golden Frogs Street is an anagram, Inspector Patrick!"

"What's an 'anagram', Dada?" asked Neil.

"An anagram is a word or phrase formed by rearranging the letters of a different word or phrase. Just like your name 'Neil' can be rearranged to form a new word 'Line'," replied Robin. After a pause, he continued, "Professor Anand had left a secret message in the form of the anagram 'H-Golden Frogs Street'. It was meant to be cryptic, so that even if someone other than the person it was meant for, sees it, he would not understand its meaning. He left this secret message for someone he deeply trusted and knew that he would be able to break the code. He left it for Syril. That is why Syril is here tonight after hearing about the cryptic message from us in the police station during the interrogation."

But what is the original phrase, Dada? What's the secret message hidden in this anagram?" asked Neil.

"Do you remember when we first came here, I had observed the bookshelf in this Drawing room very closely? It had books of almost every renowned author, but it had many books penned by a particular author whom the Professor probably liked very much. Satyajit Ray! He had English translations of almost each and every book written by him. 'H-Golden Frogs Street' is an anagram of the title of a book written by him.

The 'H-Golden Frogs Street' is actually 'The Golden Fortress', a famous novel written by the legendary Indian author, filmmaker, artist, music composer and screenwriter, Satyajit Ray," declared Robin.

"Oh God! Horo Babu, you are really a genius. I would never have been able to crack this code even in seven lifetimes! How did you do this?" Babulalji said, awestruck.

Neil and Inspector Patrick's brains were spinning. The address they were looking for since the past three days and were even considering the golden frogs of Panama for it, was actually the name of a book! They were overwhelmed by the sheer simplicity and genius of it.

"I had cracked the code yesterday morning itself with the help of Babulalji's sharp intellect," said Robin with a smile.

"My intellect? What did I do, Horo Babu?" asked a surprised Babulalji.

Robin laughed and replied, "We will discuss that later, Babulalji." He added, "I knew the Professor must have hidden something in that book and as a consequence, he lost his life for it. During Syril's and Dilip's interrogation,

I intentionally mentioned the anagram to them. Me and Inspector Patrick got the impression that Syril was familiar with the anagram, but we were not sure. The story of the killer ghost was already out in the open and I personally made sure that the news of the message left by the Professor spreads. It was just a matter of time when someone would try to get hold of that book. I decided to keep an eye on the Professor's house. Syril's response when I mentioned the Professor's secret message was suspicious, and of course, it was possible that he wouldn't come to the house tonight -- and we would have ended up keeping watch over the house for a few more days, but he came and we were saved from the labour."

Inspector Patrick thought it over for a minute and said, "But, Robin there is an extra letter in this anagram that you haven't accounted for."

"An extra letter?" queried Babulalji.

"Yes, an extra letter! If we rearrange the 'The Golden Frogs Street', we get all the letters for the phrase, 'The golden fortress', but there is an extra letter 'G' in this anagram! And where is the book, Robin? Syril did not find the book here " asked Inspector Patrick.

"Yes, you are right! And this is the part where Syril made a mistake! He cracked the secret code and deducted that it is actually an anagram which contains the name of a book, but he couldn't understand the meaning and significance of the extra letter 'G' in it. That is why he couldn't find the Professor's book even after decoding the message. Am I right, Syril?" asked Robin.

"Yes, you are right, Detective, but I thought of giving it a try, anyway. I knew the Professor had left something for me in that book, but I don't know why the book is not here," replied Syril.

Robin walked towards the bookshelf and said, "That's because you cracked only half the code, Syril! Professor Anand was a very meticulous man. If we observe this bookshelf, it is very neatly arranged alphabetically. So, 'The golden fortress' book should have been in the row 'T' of the shelf, where Syril was looking for it and did not find it. But this extra letter 'G' actually corresponds to the row 'G' of the bookshelf. The Professor intentionally kept this book in that row and very clearly mentioned it in his anagram. So, if we look in that row, we do find the book!"

Robin extended his arm and pulled out the book from the shelf. Everybody was watching him in amazement as if he was pulling a rabbit out of a hat!

Everyone's eyes in the room had widened at the sight of the book. This was the secret that Professor Anand was trying to protect from being lost forever even at the time of his death. What macabre secret did it contain that it had conjured up a ghost that had claimed not one, but two lives, and started a chain of paranormal events that were beyond human comprehension.

The secret was finally going to be revealed.

Chapter 20

Robin kept the book on a table and sat on the chair. Everybody crowded around him. There was a visible expression of tension and excitement on the faces of everyone present in the room.

It was a leather-bound book with a small locking system. Robin observed the book carefully.

"It isn't a book, but a box that has been made to look like a book and it has a lock too. We need to break it, unless Syril has something to say," Robin declared.

Syril reached into his pocket and took out a small golden key. Everyone was startled. How did he have the key to the box?

But there was something that was much more intriguing and compelling than the question at hand, so everybody chose to ignore it for the moment.

Robin took the key and slowly and carefully opened the lock. It was not a book indeed. It was a metal box that had been made to look like a book from the outside and had a small hollow space inside for storage!

Robin slowly lifted the cover. The excitement in the room was palpable and everyone was on the verge of biting into the nails of their hands.

There was a folded red-coloured piece of silk cloth similar to the one they had seen at Professor Enos' house. Robin unfolded it.

There was a small old, stained piece of leather with something embossed over it in *Devnagri* script.

And there were three antique looking gold coins.

Robin observed the coins carefully. They looked old as if belonging to the times of ancient kings and kingdoms. There was an impression of a face on one side of the coin. The face appeared to be of a king with an impressive moustache and crown. He flipped the coin. There was something written on the other side of the coin in *Devnagri script.* The scripture was very small and somewhat scuffed. Robin looked around on the table and found a magnifying glass.

He observed the coin under the magnifying glass. The scripture on the coin was now clearly visible. It read,

"To Maharaja Medini Ray, with love."

Chapter 21

"Who was Maharaja Medini Ray?" asked Neil.

Robin held the coin in his hand admiring it and replied without taking his eyes off it. He said, "I am not very proud of my knowledge of history but Maharaja Medini Ray was probably one of the most important kings in the history of Jharkhand. He was the greatest king of the Chero dynasty. He ruled the region of Palamu for thirteen years, Neil. We have a reminder of his glorious reign in the magnificent fort built by him that still exists, the Palamu Fort."

Everyone's eyes were now fixed on the coins.

"So, all this is somehow connected to the Palamu Fort and to Maharaja Medini Ray. But who is Satyabhama? Is he someone related to the king?" asked Babulalji.

"Yes, it appears so, Babulalji," replied Robin.

"Robin, we saw a similar piece of red silk cloth at Professor Enos' house, too. Did it, too, contain identical gold coins? Is the ghost of Satyabhama after these coins?

Is he killing everyone who has possession of these coins?" asked Inspector Patrick.

"It could be possible Inspector Patrick, but there is something more in this box. This small piece of leather with what appears to be a message embossed over it. Let's see," said Robin and held the magnifying glass in his hands, again.

The piece of leather appeared very old and stained. The *Devnagri* scripture over it also appeared slightly faded, but it was readable under the looking glass. Robin switched on the table lamp and tried to read it. It read,

"Where there is death among the trees due to frost,
Near the sharp fangs of Ornaga it lies lost.
Three resolute warriors guard the two friends,
Who are tormented by battles, some won some lost.
The knight who quenches the thirst of the second,
The one who holds the water of stream,
For years to come till the end of time
The elixir of Doisa is protected by him."

Robin read the scripture aloud. There was absolute silence in the room while he was reading it.

Babulalji finally broke the silence, and said, "Horo Babu, I didn't understand a word of it. What's this puzzle about? We thought these murders are due to some treasure, but now there is a mention of some 'Elixir of Doisa'. My head is spinning."

Robin turned towards Syril and asked him, "Do you know anything about this?"

"No, I don't know anything about this, Detective. I could break the code because I have had many discussions about anagrams with Professor Anand during my studies with him. He was fascinated with them. He gave me the golden key some time ago and asked me to keep it safe, but he never told me what was it for," replied Syril.

"I think he is lying again, Horo Babu! Let's check his wrist. He must be having the 'hawk' tattoo on his wrist," shouted Babulalji, excitedly.

Inspector Patrick lifted Syril's sleeves over his wrists. There was no sign of any tattoo.

Babulalji was taken aback as he was sure of finding the tattoo on his wrist. He thought for a minute, then spoke again, "But why would Professor Anand give him the key? Why would he trust him? We all know Professor Anand didn't like him and was always scolding him due to his bad habits. Then, why would he leave a secret message just for him?"

"Calm down, Babulalji. I think the Professor did trust him and I know why. But I will leave it to Syril to tell us the reason. Will you tell us, Syril?" asked Robin.

Syril was silent.

"Why Robin? What's the reason?" asked Inspector Patrick.

Robin replied in a calm voice,

"Because Professor Anand was his father."

Chapter 22

"What? Professor Anand was Syril's father?" Everybody present in the room seemed shocked at this statement. Robin and Syril were looking at each other. It appeared Syril didn't want Robin to reveal this truth. He said, "Yes, he was my father. He had married my mother in his younger days, secretly. He never told his family about her. One day, he left us. I was a small kid, then. I didn't even remember his face or name. But my mother forgave him. She said he had his reasons. She raised me alone. On the day, I took admission in St. Xavier's College for my graduation, she died due to a long illness.

Professor Anand recognized me and told me about our relationship. But I despised him. He tried to help me in every way possible, but I refused his help every time. But he never gave up on me. He continued his efforts to take care of me and scolded me for my bad habits. But despite everything, he did trust me because I was his own blood. That is why he left the message for me."

"But he never told you about these ancient gold coins and this scripture?" asked Robin.

"Maybe he tried, but I didn't listen. Since the past few weeks, he had been trying to meet me and discuss something with me, but I used to avoid him. On the night he died, he had called me, but I went there drunk. He got angry and scolded me. I left in anger not knowing that it was the last time I was going to see him alive."

There was a deep sadness on Syril's face, but there were no tears.

"Syril, whatever may be your reasons, I will have to take you into police custody for now," Inspector Patrick said.

Syril didn't say anything.

Inspector Patrick then took him into police custody. Robin asked the Inspector if he could keep the scripture on the piece of leather and one of the three gold coins with him for some time. Inspector Patrick readily agreed. The constables collected the remaining coins and took pictures of the scripture.

When the constables were taking him to the police jeep, Syril stopped near Robin and said, "I didn't kill my father, Detective."

"I know," Robin said, without looking at him.

Syril left with the constables relieved that Robin was not counting him among the murder suspects.

It was around 4:30 am when all of them finally left the Professor's house for the police station.

Robin, Babulalji and Neil were following Inspector Patrick's jeep in the Maruti 800.

"I feel as if we are stuck in the wheel of time, Horo Babu. First, a killer ghost in old, royal clothes. Then, an ancient dagger and now ancient gold coins belonging to the era of the greatest of the Chero kings, Maharaja Medini Ray along with an ancient scripture which speaks of an elixir. What is this, Horo Babu? Some kind of historical conspiracy?" asked Babulalji.

"If you feel we are stuck in the wheels of time, then enjoy the journey, Babulalji. I promise you, it's going to be one hell of a ride," replied Robin with a smile.

It took them a few minutes to reach the police station. Inspector Patrick went to complete the paperwork and asked Robin to rest in his chambers with Neil and Babulalji. He informed the commissioner about the ancient gold coins and the scripture and took permission for keeping them with Robin for some time. In the chamber, Babulalji stretched himself on the sofa. Neil drew up his chair near Babulalji and sat on it, keeping his legs stretched out on the sofa. Robin sat on another chair. They dozed off within a few minutes.

Around half an hour later, Inspector Patrick entered his chambers and woke them up, "Hey! Wake up guys and have some tea. The morning newspaper is here. You would want to see the news."

They woke up and read the news. A big headline read, 'Killer ghost loose in the city'.

There were detailed accounts of Professor Enos Baa's murder by a ghost. The news report even connected the murder of Professor Anand with it and also the police's unsuccessful attempt at covering it up. The newspapers also claimed that these incidents should not be taken as rumours as Detective Horo was also spotted around the crime scenes.

"My God! The newspapers have so many details about the two murders. Someone must be giving them information other than what we are telling them," said Inspector Patrick.

"I told you, this information will spread whatever you may do to control it. It serves someone's purpose. So, it's better not to be bothered by this," said Robin.

"Robin, I forgot to tell you that there was a special programme yesterday night on the local news channel, 'News 11'. It was named 'The revenge of a killer ghost'! What intrigued me was that it contained many details about both the murders which we have certainly not disclosed to the media. It was not possible for them to know such details. Do you think we can trace their source?" asked Inspector Patrick.

"Was 'she' the news anchor?" asked Robin.

"Yes, Robin 'she' was the news anchor!" corroborated Inspector Patrick with a smile.

"Then we can't trace their source," said Robin.

"Come on, Dada! At least give it a try. Please give it a try," said Neil in excitement.

"What's with the boy? Is he a fan?" asked Inspector Patrick looking at Neil.

"Oh the biggest!" replied Robin and continued, "Besides you know, although she is an old friend, she would never disclose her source to me, or for that matter, to anyone. She is a true crime reporter, down to her very bones!"

"Horo Babu, even I think we should give it a try. Maybe, she will tell you about her source this time considering the supernatural tones of this case," suggested Babulalji.

Robin thought of saying something in protest, but then just shrugged and gave up,

"Alright, we are going to meet Atreyi Biswas."

Chapter 23

Atreyi Biswas was one of the most prominent and fearless crime reporters that News 11 ever had in recent years. She was very well-connected and was invariably always the first to break most sensational stories.

Robin had called her and she had asked him to come to her office at 7:00 am on the seventh floor of *Panchwati* Tower at *Harmu* Road.

She came down to the canteen to meet them. She was wearing a smart black suit with a red T shirt. Neil was delighted to see her.

"Oh Babulalji and Neil, too, have come! What a surprise!" she said on seeing them together.

"Yes, Atreyi Didi, it's been a long time since I last saw you. Dada was not coming, but I insisted," complained Neil.

"Oh, he was not? Why Robin," she asked with a grin. Robin laughed.

She continued, "I know why you have come, Robin. To ask me about my source as to who is giving me the information relating to the murders committed by the killer ghost. Am I right?"

"Yes, you are right," replied Robin.

"The answer is still the same as always, Robin. I can't tell you about my source," she said.

"I understand, Atreyi. Even I didn't want to put you into this situation, but this case is a little bit complicated," said Robin.

"No, you don't understand, Robin. The reason I can't tell you is because even I don't know who he is. He personally sent someone who was clearly in disguise, and communicated only through typed notes. I am trying to find out more about him, and if I succeed, I will tell you who he is," she said.

"Very well, I'll wait for your word then," Robin said with a smile and rose from his chair.

"Robin, there is one more thing. I don't know if it is important or not, but the person who delivered me the notes had a tattoo on his wrist," said Atreyi.

"A hawk tattoo?" asked Robin.

"Yes! how did you know?" asked a surprised Atreyi.

"Long story. I will tell you later," said Robin as he took his leave after just a brief conversation with her and a cup of tea.

"This hawk tattoo is appearing too many times for

my comfort. We are being watched. We have to be very careful," said Robin looking around as they came out of the Panchwati Tower.

It was around 8:00 am now and they decided to head home as they had to work on the scripture they had found hidden in the box at Professor Anand's house. The night had been long, but fruitful.

"Horo Babu, one thing is still not clear," said Babulalji.

"What is that?" Robin asked.

"How did 'I' help you in cracking the code? You had said that you cracked the code with the help of my sharp intellect!" asked Babulalji.

"Oh that? Yesterday morning when we were sitting in the garden and you gave me the idea of re-arranging my flower pots, it occurred to me that the Professor might have done precisely the same thing. What if he had rearranged his original message to form a new phrase? His message 'H-Golden Frogs Street' was not making any sense. What if he had left a cryptic message in the form of an anagram? I tried it and it came out perfect," Robin replied.

"And I thought you were appreciating my knowledge of gardening," Babulalji said as they headed home unaware that a pair of eyes were watching them from a nearby PCO.

"He met her," said the person to someone over the phone.

"Let it be. She doesn't know anything. Besides, if we touch her, Robin will come after us like a mad dog. We don't want to make it personal for him. We don't want him mad; we want him confused," the man on the other side of the phone replied.

The man in the PCO kept the receiver down. Through his half-folded sleeve, the hawk tattoo was clearly visible on his wrist.

Chapter 24

Somra opened the gate for them as Babulalji drove the car inside.

"How was the night? Did the ghost of Satyabhama turn up at the Professor's house?" Somra asked.

"No, Somra, he didn't. But we found another puzzle. This is getting very complicated. Let's get inside. We will tell you the whole story in detail. I need a super strong cup of tea right now," Neil replied.

"Yes, in a minute, Neil. By the way, the story of the killer ghost is out in today's newspaper," Somra declared.

"Yes, we know, Somra. We read the newspaper at the police station," Robin replied.

They sat in the Drawing room and Somra brought tea for them.

"Horo Babu, have you been able to solve any part of the riddle we found at the Professor's house?" Babulalji asked.

"I have a very slight idea about some of its lines, but I need a little more information before coming to a conclusion. It is clear now that all this is connected to Maharaja Medini Ray, so we need to have a thorough knowledge of his history. We need to know if there was any mention of a treasure or some story even in the form of legends or folklore, about an 'elixir' associated with him. We need to know if there was a person with the name of Satyabhama in the recorded history of that era," Robin replied.

"Where can we get this information, Dada?" Neil asked.

"There are many sources from where we can get such information, but I want to have a chat with Professor Anil about this. I want to know what he knows and how he reacts to this puzzle," Robin replied.

"Are we going to his house today?" asked Babulalji.

"Yes, Babulalji. Get some rest. In the afternoon, we will pay him a visit," Robin replied.

Babulalji and Neil went to their rooms to get some much-needed rest. Robin sat in his library after taking his bath. He needed to brush up his knowledge of the history of Jharkhand. He called Professor Anil and asked if he could meet them at his house in the afternoon. He agreed. Robin studied for an hour and then dozed off on the recliner with a book open on his chest.

It was around 1:30 pm when Somra woke them up.

'Professor Anil must have come home from college.

He had said he would come early,' Robin thought.

They got ready and left for Professor Anil's house.

Babulalji was looking at every unknown face near their house with suspicion. His attention was focused on their wrists, as well.

"Horo Babu, do you think the people with the hawk tattoo are watching our house, too?" Babulalji asked.

"Yes, Babulalji. I think we are being watched everywhere we are going," Robin replied.

"But who are these people, Dada? Haven't you heard about them before?" Neil asked.

"I am not sure, Neil but I have a theory. In the earlier days when organized crime was prevalent in Ranchi, there were rumours of a fellow called '*Buru*' who was well-known in crime circles. Nobody had seen him, but his name was always taken in whispers among the criminal fraternity. It was said everybody feared him and his gang. But when the Ranchi police cracked down on organized crime in the city, he disappeared and his name was never heard of again," Robin replied.

"But why do you think these people with the hawk tattoo belong to his gang?" Babulalji asked.

"It's obvious, Babulalji," Robin replied looking at him.

Babulalji looked back at him puzzled and asked, "How is it obvious? It may be obvious for you, but believe me, for 'mortals' like us, it's not obvious!"

Robin laughed and said, "Alright, I will explain. Have you ever been to the *Pahari Mandir?"*

"Yes, many times. Why do you ask?" Babulalji replied.

"Very good. Do you know what that place was called before it became popular as *Pahari Mandir*?" Robin asked.

"No Horo Babu. What was it called?" Babulalji asked scratching his head.

"It was called '*Richi Buru*'. There used to be dense jungle in that area where there were plenty of hawks. *Buru* is a word in the *Mundari* language which means hawks. Because there were a large number of hawks in the area, it was called *Richi Buru*. The point of telling you this whole story is that the people who are following us have hawk tattoos on their wrists and it appears that these are members of an organized gang. So, it is possible that their tattoos denote the name Buru. Perhaps, it is the same Buru who allegedly once ruled the underworld of Ranchi and has now resurfaced. Perhaps, they are somehow involved in this case. Either they know about the so-called elixir which Professor Anand was looking for as well, and are after it, or this whole illusion of the haunting has been created by them for some reason that is still unknown to us," Robin explained.

"Dada, this affair has so many layers," Neil said.

"But, Horo Babu, in the name, *Richi Buru*, where does *Richi* come in?" Babulalji questioned.

"*Richi* was the name of a popular landowner of that time. It was taken from his name. Now no more stories,

Babulalji. We have reached Professor Anil's house," Robin said, pointing his finger towards the house.

They parked the car outside and proceeded towards Professor Anil's house.

They could not help but look at Professor Anand's house. It did look like a haunted place, now. Not even birds were sitting on its roof. In fact, there was a macabre aura surrounding it. It felt as if the house was looking back at them and asking for an explanation of the horrors it had witnessed, just a few days ago.

They ignored its silent plea and moved towards Professor Anil's house. There were questions which needed answers. There were secrets that needed to be revealed.

Chapter 25

Bheem answered the door. Professor Anil was sitting in the Drawing room. He welcomed them in and said, "I told you Robin, I was not mistaken. I knew I had seen a ghost. There is a ghost who is killing people. You were there at Professor Enos Baa's house, weren't you? You saw for yourself."

"Yes, Professor, I was there, " Robin replied.

"And that puzzle about the Golden Frogs Street? I read in the newspaper that it was a cryptic message left by Professor Anand. You never told me. When you asked me the other day about it, I thought you were looking for an address," Professor Anil said.

"Even I was not sure about the puzzle at that time, Professor," Robin replied.

"I heard Syril was caught last night at Professor Anand's house. What was he doing there? Is he involved in his murder?" Professor Anil asked.

"What do you think? Could he be involved?" Robin asked.

Professor Anil thought for a minute and replied, "Robin, he has too many bad habits and keeps even worse company, but even then, I don't think he could be involved in a crime like murder. But you never know what men are capable of."

Clearly Professor Anil was not aware of the relationship between Professor Anand and Syril. Police had refrained from sharing this information with the newspapers.

Robin said, "We are here for a different reason, Professor Anil. We have solved the puzzle of the Golden Frogs Street and have stumbled upon an ancient scripture which Professor Anand had apparently left for Syril."

"An ancient scripture? And he left it for Syril? It doesn't make sense. What is the scripture about, Robin? What does it say?" Professor Anil asked.

"We believe it is related to the Chero king of Palamu, Maharaja Medini Ray. You are a Professor of history. We were hoping you could help us understand it," Robin said.

Professor Anil looked astonished.

"Maharaja Medini Ray? He was one of the most prominent personalities in the history of Palamu and Jharkhand. He was a great king, Robin. Numerous stories of his kindness and bravery are still popular in Palamu and in nearby regions. I personally believe he was not given the importance he deserved by historians. There is very little recorded history about him, although his reign over Palamu spanned thirteen years from 1662 to 1674," he elaborated.

"You should visit the Great Palamu Fort built by him. It is magnificent! There are two forts there – one by the name of the 'Old Fort' and the other, known as 'New Fort'. He built it after defeating the King of Chhotanagpur in his capital city of Navratragadh. Unfortunately, it is in ruins now and awaits redemption by the authorities. But, certainly, as a historian, I can vouch for the scintillating history associated with Palamu and the Palamu Fort," he added.

"If properly managed and restored, perhaps it would attract more tourists and visitors than any of the forts of Rajasthan, itself," he exulted.

Professor Anil was clearly fascinated by the history of Palamu and of Maharaja Medini Ray.

He continued, "Of course, I will try and help you with the scripture as far as possible, Robin. It would be an honour. I didn't know Professor Anand was working on something this important. He never told me. When can I see the scripture and the coins, Robin?"

Robin thought something for a minute and said, "I have them with me."

Professor Anil was very excited. He said, "I can't believe I am going to see them. Let's go into my study. We'll discuss them there."

Robin, Babulalji and Neil followed him to his study on the first floor of his house. He asked them to sit on the sofa and pulled a wooden chair in front of it.

"Let's see now," Professor Anil couldn't contain his enthusiasm.

Robin took out the scripture and the ancient gold coin from a wooden box. Professor Anil held the coin in his hand very carefully and looked at it intently.

He brought a magnifying glass from his table and observed the coin under it. He saw the face of a glorious king imprinted on one side of it. He flipped it over in his palm and read out the translation of the inscription on the other side of the coin. It read, *'To Maharaja Medini Ray with love'*.

Professor Anil was thrilled. He said, looking at the coin, "Robin do you realize the significance of this coin? What I am holding in my hands right now is an extraordinary piece of history. It is evidence that validates at least one of the many folklores surrounding Maharaja Medini Ray," he said, barely able to control his excitement.

Babulalji and Neil were also very excited.

"Tell us more about it, Professor," they said.

"The very coin I have in my hand right now was once held by Maharaja Medini Ray himself! Let me tell you his story. It needs to be told, Robin."

And then the Professor started to narrate the story:

"Medini Ray's memory has withstood the test of time because of his sense of justice and kindness. A popular Hindi couplet is still spoken about him that said: 'In the reign of Raja Medini Ray, no house was without a churner and butter'. There was prosperity everywhere during his reign. It is said that he moved in disguise to learn firsthand the problems faced by his subjects and to see if any house was without a cow or a buffalo. The ones who didn't have one, were given at least one cattle on behalf of Maharaja Medini Ray. He never levied any tax on the income of his people. Once he thought of extracting at least a shell from each headman as his tribute, but each headman presented him with a gold coin instead of a normal shell as he had never demanded anything from them before!

Robin, it appears that the coin I am holding in my hands is one of those gold coins! Can you imagine? The very coins which were presented by the people to their beloved Raja Medini Ray!

This little coin has travelled more than three hundred and fifty years in time to reach us and to make us remember the extraordinary story of the person it once belonged to! Can you comprehend the beauty of this incident, Robin?" said Professor Anil, while winding up his story.

It seemed he was lost in the mists of history. Robin, Neil and Babulalji once again looked at the coin in the light of this new information. The coin somehow looked more mysterious and enigmatic than before. It was not a lifeless small piece of yellow metal anymore.

It had a story.

Chapter 26

"What about this scripture, Professor?" Robin asked.

"Yes, let's have a look at it," said Professor Anil and held the piece of the old leather very carefully in his hands. He then kept it on a small tray.

"It looks like a poem or it may be a riddle," he said looking at the scripture under the looking glass. He read aloud:

"Where there is death among the trees due to frost,
Near the sharp fangs of Ornaga it lies lost.
Three resolute warriors guard the two friends,
Who are tormented by battles, some won some lost.
The knight who quenches the thirst of the second,
The one who holds the water of stream,
For years to come till the end of time
The elixir of Doisa is protected by him"

Professor Anil read it again. He leaned back on his chair and seemed to be thinking hard of something. Robin, Babulalji and Neil were looking at him.

He said, "It does look like a riddle, but what is it about? Is there anything you know about it?"

"No, Professor. It was kept along with the coins. I have no idea what it means or from where to even start," Robin replied.

The Professor said, "It is obvious that all this is somehow connected to Raja Medini Ray. It appears Professor Anand was searching for something related to the king and he found this scripture along with the gold coins. But the lines of this riddle are not making any sense to me."

"What about the reference to the sharp fangs of Ornaga? Was there a deity or some kind of statue by this name which had sharp fangs?" Robin asked.

"No, not that I know of. Not in the recorded history of that era, at least," the Professor replied. He continued, "And if you are thinking about the third and fourth line of the riddle, then let me tell you there is no mention of any prominent 'two friends' or 'three resolute warriors' either, in the recorded history of Palamu that has survived. This scripture is obviously pointing at something very important related to the king, but Robin, I am at a loss right now. Many popular folklores are associated with Raja Medini Ray, but as far as I know, none of them mention an 'elixir'," he said.

"Is it possible that I keep these with me for today? I'll

study them and try to figure out something," he requested.

Robin readily agreed and said, "Yes, Professor. I hope you are able to help us solve this riddle. I am counting on you."

They took their leave and came out of his house.

"Horo Babu, Professor Anil gave us some really valuable information, don't you think so? He is really an intelligent person, " Babulalji said.

Robin, however, was not paying any particular attention to him. He was busy making a call, "Inspector Patrick, this is Robin. I need to ask you for something. Professor Anil must be watched at all times from now on. I want a constable to keep an eye on him and watch all his activities."

"Why Robin? What happened?" Inspector Patrick asked from the other end of the line.

Babulalji and Neil were puzzled. Why was Robin asking for surveillance over Professor Anil?

Robin replied over the phone, "I will tell you when we meet, but right now, he needs to be watched."

"Yes, yes, of course, Robin. I am sending someone there right away," Inspector Patrick said before hanging up the receiver.

"What happened, Dada? Why do you want to keep Professor Anil under surveillance?" Neil asked.

"Because I think he is somehow directly involved in this conspiracy, Neil," Robin replied.

"But why do you think so, Horo Babu? Did he not tell us everything he knew about the coins and is helping us understand the scripture too," Babulalji reasoned.

Robin looked at him and said, "Babulalji, it's quite obvious."

Babulalji rolled his eyes and said, "Horo Babu, believe me, it's not obvious for us 'mortals'!"

Robin laughed and said, "Because I never told him we had found the coins at Professor Anand's house! I told him only about the scripture and he asked for the coins too! Neither had the coins been mentioned in the newspaper reports. There was no way he could have known about the coins, unless he knew about them beforehand and was hiding that information from us."

Babulalji was perched on the bonnet of his car. With a gasp, he said, "Horo Babu, you are a genius!"

Chapter 27

"Where are we going now, Horo Babu?" Babulalji asked.

Inspector Patrick had immediately sent one of his constables in civil clothes to keep watch on the house of Professor Anil and on his movements. So, they left to concentrate on the other important aspects of the case.

"We will head home, now Babulalji. There is nothing to do for now. We will just wait and meanwhile work on the riddle at home," Robin said.

It was around 6:00 pm when they reached home.

Somra was busy putting up the badminton net in the garden.

"Wow! Are we having a badminton match, today?" asked Neil.

"The weather was good, so I thought you would enjoy the game," Somra said.

Babulalji and Robin were excellent badminton players

and they often played matches at Robin's house.

Somra brought tea for them. Robin and Babulalji started playing. Neil was watching them play sitting on the easy chair and Somra sat on the steps of the porch.

"So Horo Babu, tell us what have you figured out about the riddle till now?" Babulalji asked Robin while hitting a clear shot towards him.

Robin returned the shot with a powerful drive shot aimed towards Babulalji's head, who ducked just on time.

"I don't think I am in my flow today, Horo Babu. I am distracted because of the puzzle," Babulalji said.

"Yes, you are right, Babulalji. Let's sit and discuss about the puzzle, instead," Neil added.

"Alright, whatever you say," Robin said and sat on the easy chair.

He continued, "I did some study when we came back from Professor Anand's house today morning and tried to figure out the puzzle. At least some part of it. To begin with, we have to decide what this puzzle is about. What do we get when we solve the puzzle? What is the prize?"

"The elixir of Doisa?" Neil said hesitantly.

"Very true, Neil. This riddle has been written to encode the location of the 'elixir of Doisa'. That means Professor Anand was on a quest to find the elixir of Doisa," Robin said.

"A real elixir? The key to immortality? Does such a thing exist?" Babulalji asked.

"We will come to that later, Babulalji. Let's come to the first line of the riddle:

Where there is death among the trees due to frost'

This sentence obviously refers to the place where the elixir is kept. We know all this mess is connected to the history of Palamu so we should start at Palamu itself. This brings us to the question:

Where is death among the trees in Palamu?" Robin asked.

Neil and Babulalji shrugged.

"Very well. Do you know the origin of the name Palamu?" he asked them.

Neil and Babulalji gave him blank looks.

Robin smiled and said, "Palamu is derived from the Hindi word, *palna* meaning a place of refuge. But there is one more theory about the origin of its name. It says Palamu is a combination of two words. First *pala* meaning frost and second *mu* that means dead. So, these two words when used together mean 'dead due to frost'! It was probably named because of the extreme winter temperatures there.

'Among the trees' may refer to the dense jungles of Palamu. So, the first sentence of the riddle implies that the elixir of Doisa is in the jungles of Palamu itself! Am I making any sense to you?"

"Yes, Dada. Your deduction is just brilliant!" Neil replied gazing at his elder cousin with admiration.

Robin continued, "Now we come to the second sentence of the riddle,

'Near the sharp fangs of Ornaga, it lies lost'.

I haven't figured out this, yet. My guess is that it refers to some statue with fangs. We'll work on it later, but it means the elixir is lying hidden somewhere near the statue with fangs or whatever it is," he said.

"Let's proceed to the next two sentences now,

'Three resolute warriors guard the two friends,
Who are tormented by battles, some won some lost'

I am not very sure about these two lines either, but during the Mughal invasion of Palamu by Daud Khan in 1660, Anant Ray who was the king of Palamu then, fought together with his relative Pratap Ray. Perhaps the 'two friends' mentioned in the riddle are Anant Ray and Pratap Ray. I am still in the dark about who the 'three warriors' are in the riddle. I couldn't find any mention of these warriors anywhere in the history books. But I find these sentences odd within the riddle, as they do not indicate the place where the elixir is hidden," he explained to his audience of three, who were listening in rapt attention.

"Maybe they refer to the time or year when the elixir was hidden. Perhaps in the reign of Anant Ray?" suggested Babulalji.

"Perhaps, but I still feel it is a bit odd," Robin replied and continued,

"Let's take up the rest of the lines,

'The knight who quenches the thirst of the second.
The one who holds the water of stream.
For years to come till the end of time
The elixir of Doisa is protected by him'

I may be wrong, but given the circumstances, 'the knight' in the riddle in all possibility seems to be Satyabhama himself! If we assume that Professors Anand and Enos Baa were after the elixir of Doisa, then it is Satyabhama who is coming to protect it and even killing people for it. That may be the curse Professor Anand was referring to — that if someone tries to acquire the elixir, the ghost of Satyabhama punishes them! And in all probability, the elixir is hidden near his grave or his final resting place."

"But what about the lines referring to the knight who quenches the thirst of the second and the one who holds the water of stream?" Neil asked.

"This one, too, I have not been able to solve still, Neil," Robin replied and then continued, "Now we come to the 'elixir of Doisa'. There was a reason that made me suspect Professor Anil is hiding something. Because he said he didn't know anything about the 'elixir of Doisa' although in an earlier conversation, he had mentioned that Raja Medini Ray had defeated the king of Chhotanagpur in his capital city of 'Navratragadh'."

"What does Navratragadh have to do with Doisa? Now please don't say it's obvious! Because it's not," Babulalji said excitedly.

Robin laughed and replied, "It has everything to do with Doisa. Because the Navratragadh as we know it today, was known by the name of 'Doisa' in the time of the Chero dynasty rule over Palamu!"

He paused and continued: "Professor Anil is a historian and must have known this fact, but he pretended that he didn't. That means he tried to conceal this information from us."

"Horo Babu, it feels like a spider's elaborate web now! How are you even processing these leads?" Babulalji said, while scratching his head.

Robin smiled and continued, "Now we come to the most important part of the mystery. Listen very carefully, both of you. What is the 'Elixir of Doisa'? Does it refer to a real elixir which gives us immortality?"

Babulalji, Neil and Somra asked at the same time, in unison, "Does it?"

"No! Not by a long shot," Robin replied and added, "It is said that when Raja Medini Ray defeated the Raja of Chhotanagpur in his capital city of Doisa, he got hold of its priceless treasure. The treasure of Doisa was said to be incredibly rich with billions in worth of gold, silver, diamonds, precious stones and ornaments! With this treasure that he had acquired from Doisa, he built the Palamu Fort and used it to spread prosperity everywhere in his kingdom. It was said that the 'treasure' of Doisa acted like an 'elixir' for the Chero dynasty. But the treasure was so vast that Raja Medini Ray could spend only a small part of it. The rest, he hid in a secret place. He probably wanted to use it later for the wellbeing of the people of Palamu."

Robin let this sink in and then, added, "It is said that the treasure was never heard of again. It was forgotten with the passage of time. The few confidantes of Raja Medini Ray who knew about its location died or perhaps were killed for it and they took that secret to their grave. Raja Medini Ray too never disclosed its location as he learnt that his ministers were plotting a conspiracy against his family in a bid to find out the location of the hidden treasure."

The three couldn't wait for Robin to continue.

"It is documented in the history of Palamu that after Raja Medini Ray died, there was a sudden rise in conspiracies in his court against his family and his successor and that this finally led to the downfall of the Chero dynasty. Some historians believe it was because of the lost treasure of Doisa. So, we reach the conclusion, my dear friends, that the 'elixir of Doisa' is actually the unfathomably rich 'treasure' left behind by the greatest of the Chero kings, Maharaja Medini Ray!" said Robin with his characteristic flourish.

"Even the British had heard about the treasure. When its armies invaded Palamu, they searched for the treasure, but couldn't find it. The treasure is still hidden somewhere in Palamu waiting for someone to discover it. It has been lying hidden for more than three hundred and fifty years for someone to come and find it!" Robin had finally completed his fascinating narrative.

His audience now had their mouths agape with wonder and amazement. They were completely bewildered by what

Robin had said just now.

"You mean Professors Anand, Enos Baa, Anil and the people with the hawk tattoo — all are after the treasure? And this riddle that we found at Professor Anand's house points to the exact location of it?" Babulalji asked.

Robin lifted his cup of tea and took a sip. He replied calmly, "Yes, Babulalji. This is no longer a mere tangled ghost story. This is a treasure hunt and we are the Treasure Hunters!"

Chapter 28

There was an absolute stunned silence in the garden. Neil, Babulalji and Somra were still trying to digest the fact that an unimaginably rich and incredibly valuable treasure was still hidden somewhere in a forest at Palamu.

"Dada, this is incredible! In school, I have always hated my history books. I never thought history could be this interesting. We are in a quest to find a lost treasure," Neil said in excitement.

"But Horo Babu, we have still solved only half of the riddle. We know the treasure is hidden somewhere in Palamu. But where? Palamu is a big area. Besides, there still remains the unexplained mystery of Satyabhama's ghost. How do we untangle this mystery?" Babulalji said.

"Babulalji, it's time to call in our fourth musketeer. We have to plan a trip to Palamu. There is no way we are going to solve this mystery without exploring the place of its origin. Make the call, Neil," Robin said.

Babulalji was delighted. Neil was happy too — not only because they were going for a trip to Palamu, but also because he was going to meet their fourth musketeer after a long time.

Neil made the call from the Drawing room and returned back to the garden.

"He will be here, tomorrow morning. And he is bringing his caravan!" he said happily.

Robin whistled the tune of the legendary theme of the 1966 Hollywood blockbuster *"The Good, the Bad and the Ugly"* composed by the Italian composer Ennio Morricone and said with a smile,

"I thought he would come riding a horse!"

Chapter 29

1669 AD
Palamu, Jharkhand

It was the night of the full moon and Satyabhama was riding towards the old mosque built outside the upper fort on his black stallion. The poor orphan boy from the village was now the head of the Maharaja's Royal Guards. He had a formidable personality and he commanded authoritative respect among all ranks of the Maharaja's army.

'Why has the king called me at this hour of the night outside the fort? He has not been keeping well these days. I hope he is all right, ' he said to himself. He was worried for his King.

He saw a human figure clad in a black blanket, carrying an oil-lamp in his hand outside the old mosque. The figure swung the lamp twice as if to signal to him. Satyabhama sped towards the mosque. It took his muscular black stallion only a few minutes to reach the old mosque, built a few kilometers outside the gate of the upper fort.

He dismounted from his horse and tied the animal to a pillar outside the mosque. The figure carrying the oil lamp was none other than Commander Trishul Singh.

He escorted Satyabhama inside. Raja Medini Ray was standing at the window of the mosque with his back towards him. He was also wearing a black robe over his clothes. The mosque was lit by another small lamp.

The king asked Satyabhama to come in. Maharaja Medini Ray was looking tired and weary. He said, "I had to call you at this hour of the night, Satyabhama, because I am worried about my people. There are poisonous snakes all around in my kingdom in the guise of greedy ministers and officers. They have been plotting against my family."

He continued, sounding weary and dejected, "The irony is that they are not doing it for the throne. They are doing it for money. They want to rob the wealth of Palamu. They are constantly feeding lies to my family members who are in the line of the throne and instigating them to turn against each other. They want this empire to fall so that they can lay their hands on a few pieces of silver and run away."

"I know my Lord," Satyabhama said.

"So far, with the help of Commander Trishul Singh and you, we have been able to foil their plots, but I don't know for how long we can keep this up. Do you know what they are after?" Raja Medini Ray asked.

"Yes, my Lord, they are after the elixir of Doisa," Satyabhama replied.

"Yes, Satyabhama, they are after the priceless treasure we won at the battle of Doisa. But it belongs to the people of Palamu. We can't let them have it. It should be used for the welfare of my kingdom. The time has come to hide it, Satyabhama — at some very secret place which would be known only to the three of us. Can you do it for me, son?" the king asked.

"You need only ask, my lord. I can give my life for you," Satyabhama replied.

The Maharaja was overwhelmed by those words. He remembered their first meeting when Satyabhama was a simple, sixteen-year-old, thin village boy. He was very proud of him.

"Do you have any suggestions where we can hide it?" Trishul Singh asked Satyabhama.

"Yes, I have, Sir. But we can't simply hide a treasure that big without anybody arousing suspicion. We will need decoys," Satyabhama said.

"Decoys? What do you mean?" Trishul Singh asked.

"We should start some random construction projects all around our kingdom. Houses for poor people. Maybe, even community halls. We could do some random renovation in the old and new forts, too. And when the people begin looking at all this construction as routine, I will hide the treasure somewhere at a site of our choice in Palamu with the help of our own people."

"This does sound like a good plan," the king said in appreciation.

"But, my Lord…" Satyabhama hesitated.

"What is it, son? Tell me," the king said.

"To make it look convincing and genuine, we need to take some drastic steps. We need to brick up and close the Nagpuri Gate of the new fort," Satyabhama said.

The king and Trishul Singh looked at each other in surprise.

The king thought for a moment and said, "You do know that I have imported the beautiful *Nagpuri gate* at great expense as I really love its beautiful carvings."

"Yes, I do, my Lord," Satyabhama replied immediately.

"And still you want me to brick it up?" he asked again.

"Yes, my lord," Satyabhama replied again without hesitating.

The king looked straight into his eyes for a minute. Satyabhama did not flinch. There was no hesitation at all or any hint of uncertainty in his eyes. He knew what he was doing. The king nodded his head in surrender, and said, "Very well, then. Do what you want. Brick it up! But everybody knows my love and admiration for the Nagpuri gate. What reason are we going to give to the people for closing it?"

Satyabhama replied with composure, "We can spread the rumour that the side of the fort wall in which the gate is located is proving to be unlucky, so we need to change the direction of the entrance to the fort. We can blame it all on *vaastu dosh* my Lord!"

Maharaja Medini Ray laughed, "Yes, indeed. We can do that. Trishul Singh give the boy whatever he needs. He is now the 'protector' of the Elixir of Doisa."

For the next one year, they worked relentlessly on this crusade of protecting and hiding the treasure of Doisa. The great Nagpuri gate was bricked up without any questions, and the great treasure of the king of Palamu was hidden away at a secret place known only to a few.

But the snakes and traitors in the Maharaja's kingdom never stopped searching for it. They were hell bent on destroying the Chero dynasty and robbing it of its spoils.

Chapter 30

Babulalji woke up from his sleep. He was feeling thirsty. They had gone to sleep early tonight. He looked at Neil who was fast asleep on the sofa, then looked at the clock. It was 11:00 pm. He had forgotten to keep a bottle of water in his room, so he went to take a bottle from the small refrigerator in Robin's library.

He turned to go back when he heard the spine-chilling howl of a dog. His attention strayed to the gibbous moon that could be seen outside the large glass window above the stairs that led to the terrace. Suddenly, the phone rang! He was so startled that the bottle fell to the floor.

Robin and Neil woke up by the noise and came out of their rooms. Robin picked up the phone. It was Inspector Patrick.

He asked Robin to come to Professor Anil's house as soon as possible.

"But why? What happened?" Robin asked.

"Satyabhama has attacked Professor Anil!" Inspector Patrick replied.

"What? Is he dead?" Robin asked.

"No, he is alive. Our constable who was watching him and the house, saved him," he replied.

"I am coming," Robin said and kept the receiver down.

"What happened, Horo Babu? What did he say?" Babulalji asked.

"Satyabhama's ghost has attacked Professor Anil. The constable fortunately reached him on time and was able to save his life. We have to go, " Robin replied and asked them to get ready quickly.

Babulalji's heart sank. He thought, 'All this just cannot be an illusion. The threat is real. The ghost is real. And instead of running away from it, Horo Babu takes us there every time. It won't be long before the ghost comes for us!'

A few minutes later, they were heading to Professor Anil's house in the Maruti car.

"Horo Babu, Satyabhama must have attacked Professor Anil because of the ancient coin and scripture he had kept with him today. What if we had brought them home? He would have attacked us!" Babulalji said in fright.

"Yes, it appears so, Babulalji," Robin agreed.

"Dada, we were earlier thinking that Professor Anil is involved in this conspiracy, but he himself is being attacked by the ghost. We were so wrong about him," Neil said.

Robin didn't say anything. He was thinking. When

they reached the Professor's house, Inspector Patrick was waiting for them outside.

"What happened, Inspector Patrick?" Robin asked.

"Robin, it is only because of your request of keeping watch on Professor Anil that he is alive today. Our constable whom I had assigned to keep an eye on the Professor saw him getting attacked by Satyabhama and saved him," Inspector Patrick said.

"The constable saw him getting attacked? He saw the ghost?" Robin asked.

"Yes, he did! He will tell you the whole story," Inspector Patrick said as he called the constable.

"Did you see the ghost?" Robin asked the constable.

"Yes, Mr. Robin, I saw him," the constable replied.

"I was keeping watch on Professor Anil. I wanted to have a cigarette, so I went to the nearby tea stall to get a matchbox. When I returned, I saw the Professor standing in his front balcony. I think he was drinking because he had a glass in his hand. Suddenly, I saw white smoke coming out from the door which opened into his balcony. Before I could do anything, a mysterious figure dressed in royal clothes appeared in the balcony. He had emerged out of the smoke! I could not see him properly, because I was far away, but it appeared that he had a dagger in his hand. His arms were ablaze with a blueish fire. I ran towards the Professor's house. He saw me running towards him. I shouted and indicated that he should look behind. He turned and saw the ghost who was about to attack him with the dagger. He screamed and jumped from the balcony. I jumped over his boundary gate and reached him. He suffered only some minor bruises as he had jumped over the grass in the lawn. I looked up to the balcony, but the ghost had disappeared in the smoke. I tried to open the door of his house and knocked hard. Bheem opened the door. He was sleeping in the kitchen and was not aware of what had just happened.

When he saw Professor Anil lying in the lawn, he ran outside. I went running up to the balcony, but there was nothing there. Just the dissipating smoke and a strange smell...the smell of garlic," the constable said.

Inspector Patrick said, "Then he came down to the garden, and with Bheem's help, he brought the Professor inside and called me."

Robin was still thinking. He asked, "Where is the Professor?"

"He is sitting in his study," said Inspector Patrick and gestured to them that they follow him. He went to Professor Anil's study.

A constable was standing outside the door talking to the forensic team. He had a transparent polythene bag in his hand containing the beautiful golden dagger that was similar to the ones used to kill both the Professors - Anand as well as Enos Baa.

Inspector Patrick showed them the dagger and said, "This one too is exactly the same as the other two daggers. We found it in the balcony. Maybe, it fell off the ghost's hands."

Robin saw the dagger. True, it was an identical copy of the other two used in the previous murders.

They went inside the study and found the Professor sitting on a chair. He saw them and said in a tone marked by despair, "He came to kill me, Robin. The ghost. He was so scary! I am alive because of a policeman who was passing by. The coin is really cursed. The ghost will kill anyone who is in possession of the coin! That was what happened to Professor Anand and Professor Enos."

Robin held both his shoulders, and said, "Calm down, Professor. He is gone now. We will take the coin and the scripture with us. You will be safe. Inspector Patrick will arrange for your security."

He continued, "Now, please tell me what exactly happened."

Professor Anil looked at him and replied, "I was studying the riddle and trying to figure it out with the help of some books. I got tired and went to the balcony to get some fresh air. I was having tea when I saw a man running towards my house. I was surprised. He shouted and gestured to me to look behind. When I turned, I saw the ghost of Satyabhama who was about to attack me with the golden dagger. I couldn't think of any other way to escape and instinctively jumped from the balcony. Fortunately, I fell on the grass in the lawn and didn't suffer any major injuries."

Robin asked Bheem too about what had happened. He said he didn't know anything about it. He was sleeping in the kitchen. He got up because someone was banging on the door. He opened it to find the police constable bending over Professor Anil who was lying on the ground outside.

"Robin, I am really sorry, but I don't think I want to keep the coin and the riddle with me in this house. I think they are really haunted," Professor Anil said in a shaky voice.

Robin said, "That's fine, Professor. We will take them back with us." Robin picked up the coin and the riddle embossed on a piece of leather from his table.

"But Robin, I have made a copy of the riddle. I will try to solve it and inform you if I do," Professor Anil said.

"Where is the copy? Can I see it?" Robin asked.

"Yes, of course. It's right there at the corner of the table." He pointed his fingers towards it.

Robin saw the copy of the riddle at the corner of the table. The Professor had written it on a piece of paper with black ink. He stretched his hand to pick it up.

Just when he was about to touch the paper, it caught fire spontaneously!

Robin withdrew his hand at once. Everybody in the room was shocked and knocked speechless.

The piece of paper burnt away in a white smoke and smelt of garlic.

Everyone in the room froze with fear. They couldn't believe their eyes.

"The ghost doesn't want anybody to solve the mystery, Horo Babu," Babulalji said. His eyes were wide with fear.

Inspector Patrick was looking at Robin in amazement.

'How can even Robin explain this? This is certainly a work of some ungodly supernatural power, ' he thought.

Robin was silent. He was looking at the reddish black ash residue of the burnt paper.

It appeared these strange happenings were shaking his faith in reality. Was he too beginning to believe in the existence of ghosts?

The police and the forensic team were busy looking for evidence in the house. Bheem was sitting near the Professor on the floor. He was looking terrified.

Robin asked Inspector Patrick to come outside to the lawn. Neil and Babulalji were watching them from a distance. Robin was explaining something, but Inspector Patrick did not appear to be convinced.

"What are they talking about, Babulalji?" Neil asked.

"I think Horo Babu must be still trying to convince him that this is not a work of a ghost but some illusion and Inspector Patrick must be presenting an argument against it," Babulalji replied.

They saw Inspector Patrick call someone over the phone. After around five minutes, they came back inside the house.

Professor Anil was not looking well. Inspector Patrick got him admitted to the nearby '*Harmu* Hospital and Research Centre' for observation. Bheem stayed with him in the hospital.

After getting the Professor admitted and arranging for his security, Inspector Patrick, Robin, Babulalji and Neil stood in silence outside the hospital. The night was lit by the blueish light of the gibbous moon.

Inspector Patrick asked, "Are we going to survive this, Robin? I don't even know how to say this that a ghost is attacking and killing people right below our noses despite our best efforts. The press is going to burn our effigy! We have no logical explanation of the bizarre things we are encountering in this case. The copy of the riddle caught fire spontaneously in front of our eyes! A similar thing happened at Professor Enos' house with the curtains. The statements made by Bheem and Professor Anil in connection with Professor Anand's murder seem to be nothing short of a Halloween tale."

He added, "Now even my constable has seen the ghost who just appeared out of smoke and then dissipated back into it!"

He turned to Robin and said: "In my opinion, I don't think a petty criminal would attempt these attacks repeatedly when the police is on its toes to catch the culprit. I don't think he would take this high risk of getting caught. It is being done by someone who is beyond the police and the law. It is being done by a ghost, Robin."

Robin said to himself: 'This has certainly not been done by some petty criminal. '

Inspector Patrick yawned and said, "I need caffeine, Robin. I have a headache. I am going to have some tea. Do you want to join me?"

"No, Inspector Patrick, we'll head for home," Robin said.

"Horo Babu, I was thinking — is it necessary to take the coin and the riddle home with us? Can't we give it back to Inspector Patrick?" Babulalji asked in a whisper.

Robin smiled and said, "We are taking them home, Babulalji."

Babulalji was not at all happy with Robin's reply but he didn't say anything.

They reached home. Robin kept the coin and the riddle in his room. Babulalji went to sleep in Neil's room, but both were very worried, thinking, 'The night is still young, and now the cursed coin is in the house! What if the ghost of Satyabhama comes for us? Why is Robin not worried about the two artifacts? Does he know something that they don't?'

There were too many questions that needed answers. Soon the burden of those questions sat heavy on their eyelids and they dozed off unaware of the two dark shadows lurking just inside their boundary wall.

Chapter 31

Neil woke up by the sound of a loud horn. He looked at the clock on the side table near the sofa on which he was sleeping. It was 7:30 am. Babulalji was fast asleep on Neil's bed and was snoring.

'It must be some large vehicle passing by,' he thought to himself, and settled back to sleep some more.

He heard the clanging of the large boundary gate being opened.

'Someone is here early,' he told himself.

And then it struck him, "Has he come already?" He jumped out of the sofa and ran towards the window. He saw Somra opening the gate for a cream-and-brown coloured caravan to enter the compound of the house. The 'fourth musketeer' had arrived!

Neil was excited. He shook Babulalji awake.

"Babulalji, wake up! Naseem Bhai is here!"

Babulalji woke up rubbing his eyes.

"He is here already?"

Neil ran out of the room to the garden to greet him.

The caravan was being parked in the courtyard. Robin was already sitting in the garden.

Naseem Bhai disembarked from his caravan. He was looking like someone straight out of a Clint Eastwood cowboy movie! He was 5 feet 8 inches tall and had a dusky complexion. He was wearing a blue-check shirt with boot-cut, faded jeans. His cowboy look was complete with a brown hat, black aviators, a brown belt with an eagle's head-shaped buckle and pointed, brown leather shoes. He had a typical habit of keeping a matchstick in between his lips and capering with it.

He jumped out of the driving seat and said with a typical Clint Eastwood kind of accent, "Do ya' feel lucky, punk?"

Robin laughed and shook his hand, "Welcome, Naseem Bhai. It's always good to see you."

Naseem Bhai was the owner of the famous Naseem's Garage at Kanke block. He had started the garage when he was merely a teenager and had worked very hard to establish it as a well-known garage in Ranchi. Being the eldest of three brothers, he now only handled the managerial aspect of the business while most of the work was done by his younger siblings.

He was a die-hard Clint Eastwood fan. He had watched all his movies multiple times, specially his Wild West movies and had remembered every dialogue by the legendary film star and would somehow weave them into the conversation whenever he got the chance. He loved dressing up like a cowboy and with his love for Eastwood quotes, he was known among his friends as the 'Cowboy of Kanke'!

He had known Robin since he was a kid. Robin's father had supported him like his own son when he was struggling and that was the reason why he felt a very strong bond for Robin.

Whenever Robin worked on a case where he had to go out of the city, he would call Naseem Bhai.

Neil ran towards him and gave him a tight hug.

"Naseem Bhai, we were asking Robin Dada to call you sooner, but he did not listen."

Naseem laughed and said, "Don't worry, Neil. Now I am here. When is our adventure going to begin?"

Robin replied, "Hopefully tomorrow morning, Naseem Bhai. I am planning to leave for Palamu early morning tomorrow."

"Yes, Robin. That's fine by me. But tell me the whole story first. What are we looking for?" he asked.

Robin narrated to him the whole story about the ghost of Satyabhama and the murders committed by him, the people with the hawk tattoos, the ancient gold coins and the riddle about the treasure and how it was somehow connected to the Palamu Fort.

Naseem Bhai was amazed by the story. He said, "I

think this is going to be fun! Is the 'Tornado' with us?"

"Yes, the 'Tornado' is here, Naseem Bhai," Babulalji said with a smile. He had come out into the garden.

"Now that our team is complete, I don't think the ghost stands a chance!" Neil said happily.

They laughed and went inside the house. Somra cooked a nice breakfast for them. Most of the day went in planning and preparing for the Palamu trip. Babulalji tried to bring up the issue of the ancient coin and the riddle lying inside the house, and the possibility of an attack by the ghost of Satyabhama, but Robin did not pay much attention to it.

Somra's nephew, Tulsi Oraon lived at Palamu. He said Tulsi would be able to help them when they reached Palamu as he knew the area and could take them to the Palamu Fort. They agreed to the offer readily. Somra called Tulsi to alert him.

Tulsi asked to be picked up from the *Van Vihar* Hotel at *Betla*, as he was out of Palamu and was reaching the hotel in the morning.

Naseem Bhai said it wasn't far off their route so they could easily pick him up.

Somra informed Tulsi and asked him to be there in the morning.

The sun slowly faded away, paving the way for the kingdom of the night to take over. The lively atmosphere inside the house was opposite of the grim aura of the night outside.

Babulalji had managed to convince them to sleep together in the hall. After dinner, they spread mattresses on the floor. Robin slept on the sofa while Neil, Babulalji and Naseem Bhai took the mattresses.

Somra too had spread his mattress near the dining table in the hall.

In the dim light of the night bulb, they were discussing the riddle. Robin was still uncertain about the lines that referred to the 'fangs of Ornaga' and the lines that mentioned something about 'quenching the thirst of the second' and 'holding the water of the stream'.

Naseem Bhai said, "It does seem that there may be a statue named 'Ornaga' with sharp fangs and that the treasure may be hidden near it. It is even possible that the statue may have been there once but it is not there anymore. I mean it has been more than three hundred and fifty years since the time of Maharaja Medini Ray."

He told them that he had been to the Palamu Forts a few years back.

"There was no statue in either of the forts. Logically, it would have been impossible to hide the treasure in the fort itself as there would have been lots of people at the fort all the time. So, it must be hidden somewhere outside the fort. There are ruins of the old town to the south of the upper fort. Perhaps, we should look there," he said.

Robin said, "Yes, you are right, Naseem Bhai, the treasure could be anywhere at Palamu. But we must locate it so that we can catch the people who are involved in these mysterious murders."

"What about the fifth and sixth lines of the riddle, Robin Dada?" Neil asked.

"I am not sure about them, Neil. That is why I have planned this trip to Palamu. Perhaps, we will get a new perspective after visiting the place," Robin replied.

"It's quite late and we must get some sleep. We have to leave early in the morning," Babulalji said and rose up to fetch a bottle of water from the table.

While he was drinking water, his eyes wandered towards the window of the hall. He saw something. His eyes widened with fear and his blood froze in his veins. He shuddered, but could not move. All of them saw his facial expression and turned their gaze towards the window.

The threat had come home.

There was someone outside their window. It was dark outside and the person at the window was not clearly visible, but he seemed to be dressed in old and tattered royal clothes and was limping slowly towards the window.

"S… Satyabhama… his ghost has come…," Babulalji stammered in a voice filled with fear.

Robin jumped out of the sofa and ran towards the front door.

It was locked.

Somra had locked all the doors before going to sleep.

"Get the keys," Robin shouted.

He looked at the window again. The shadow had disappeared. Somra opened the front door and Robin and

Naseem Bhai ran out. There was nobody outside. Babulalji, Neil and Somra followed them. Robin and Naseem Bhai then ran towards the back of the house. There was nobody in the compound. Robin jumped and climbed over the boundary wall. He could not see anyone outside, either.

Babulalji was panicking. "Horo Babu, I told you not to keep the coins and the riddle with us. The ghost of Satyabhama has come for them!" Babulalji said, shivering with fear.

"Relax Babulalji. He is gone," Robin replied.

Just as Robin said these words, the smell of garlic spread in the air.

Neil looked at Robin with fear in his eyes.

And the curtains near the porch burst into flames!

Everybody was stunned. Babulalji fainted. Naseem Bhai caught him just in time.

Somra was dumbstruck at first, but then he realized the gravity of the situation and ran towards the garden hose and turned it towards the burning curtains.

Neil too was shell-shocked.

Robin looked at Naseem Bhai who was holding Babulalji trying to rouse him. He was still capering with a matchstick in between his lips.

Suddenly, in that most unusual moment Robin realized something. He had found the missing piece of the puzzle that had been bothering him. Something he had missed before.

Naseem Bhai who was completely unaware of what was going-on in Robin's mind, asked him, "Are you sure he is not a real ghost? He seemed pretty real to me."

Chapter 32

"You saw the ghost this time with your own eyes, Robin?" Inspector Patrick asked. Robin had called him immediately after the ghost sighting.

"No, I didn't see him properly. It was dark outside. I just saw a shadow at the window," Robin replied.

"Horo Babu, how can you deny it? We all saw him. It was dark, but we could make out that he was wearing tattered, ancient clothes. He was the ghost of Satyabhama! If he was a man, then how did he disappear all of a sudden? You and Nassem Bhai both searched for him in the compound, but didn't find anyone. What about the curtains which spontaneously ignited? This is some dangerous curse, Horo Babu. This is strong black magic! Satyabhama was here to fulfill the curse and to take the coin and the riddle with him," Babulalji said, sounding completely distraught.

"Did he take the coin and the riddle?" Inspector Patrick asked.

"No, he disappeared when Robin tried to open the door," Naseem Bhai replied.

"It's good that nobody was hurt. Do you want me to take the coin and the riddle back with me?" Inspector Patrick asked.

"No, let it be with me for some more time," Robin replied.

Babulalji looked at Neil disapprovingly, but he didn't say anything.

The forensic team completed their routine investigation but they found nothing. Inspector Patrick left at around 3:00 am.

"Is our Palamu trip still on?" Neil asked.

"Yes, it is on. Let's get some sleep. We have to start early in the morning," Robin replied.

They lay down again, but Babulalji did not let anybody turn off the lights of the hall. Nobody objected. They knew Babulalji was frightened out of his wits.

It was 7:30 am, when Babulalji woke up. He saw Robin, Naseem Bhai and Neil sitting under the porch. They had let him sleep as they wanted him to get some rest.

He thought of the events of the last night. 'Was it a nightmare?' he wondered. But he knew, it was not. He had experienced a real haunting last night. He went outside.

"Babulalji, you are awake. Did you get good sleep?" Naseem Bhai asked.

"Yes, I slept somehow, although I was thinking I won't

be able to. But you should have woken me up. We will be late for our trip," said Babulalji.

"That's fine, Babulalji. You needed some rest after the events of last night. Now get ready. We will leave as soon as possible. If we reach Palamu very late, we will just stay at the *Van Vihar* hotel itself at *Betla,* from where we have to pick up Tulsi and visit the fort, the next day. What do you say, Naseem Bhai?" Robin asked.

"Yes, Robin. We will take the Ranchi – Kuru – Latehar – Daltonganj route. It will take us a little more than five hours to reach Palamu if we don't make too many unscheduled stops during the journey. So, it's better we start early," Naseem Bhai replied.

"What are we waiting for? We should get ready," Robin said.

They went inside. Somra prepared some snacks and tea for them to keep in the caravan.

It was around 9:00 am when they embarked on their journey — a journey that was either going to clear the dust of time from many a lost secret or was going to expose them to some deadly ancient truths.

Robin had kept the coin and the riddle with him, but didn't tell Babulalji anything connected to it as he knew that Babulalji would panic after knowing about the two objects being in the caravan.

Their journey was pleasant as they passed through the beautiful and captivating terrain of 'Nature's hidden jewel', Jharkhand.

Naseem Bhai was driving the caravan on beautiful roads lined by trees on both sides as they crossed Kuru. Robin sat next to Naseem Bhai. Babulalji and Neil occupied the back seats.

It was a comfortable caravan with arrangements for sleeping and it had a small bathroom, too. On the way they crossed the huts of many local people who were busy with their daily activities. There was a group of villagers who were standing in front of a 'Bolero'. One of them waved at their caravan. Neil waved back at him.

"Nice village people," he remarked.

Robin looked at him and smiled.

They saw many vehicles of armed special forces too as they entered Latehar. The forces had been arranged for by the government to ensure the safety of the people.

Somra had packed lots of flasks of tea and ample snacks for them to savour during their journey.

They reached *Daltonganj* and saw a large overhead green board which read, '*Betla* 13 km'. The road to the right led to *Daltonganj* town and the one on the left, led to *Betla.* They took the left turn and headed towards *Betla*, passing through a beautiful, arched gate. A few kilometers drive from the gate brought them to a small bridge built near the beautiful confluence of North *Koel* and *Auranga* rivers known popularly as *Kechki.*

Robin asked Naseem Bhai to stop so that they could stretch their limbs and spend some time absorbing the beauty of the place. Neil took out his camera and clicked pictures.

Naseem Bhai stood in front of the caravan leaning on it.

"Robin, I wanted to ask you a question, even though I know you must be having some reason for it which we are not able to comprehend right now," Naseem Bhai remarked.

"What is it, Naseem Bhai? What's bothering you?" Robin asked.

"What I have observed and what Babulalji has been repeatedly telling me is that you are hell bent on proving that the murders are not committed by a ghost, but are a result of a conspiracy by someone. Do you know something that we don't? Because what I saw last night was something that did not belong to our world," Naseem Bhai said.

Robin replied in a calm voice, "Naseem Bhai, you have been carrying the answer to this question all along in between your lips!"

Naseem Bhai was surprised.

"In between my lips? What? Does it have something to do with this matchstick?" he asked.

Robin smiled and said, "Don't worry, Naseem Bhai even I realized this last night only. Let's go. Hotel *Van Vihar* is not far from here."

Naseem Bhai scratched his head in confusion and then nodded his head in submission.

'Why did I even ask him? Nothing he says makes any sense ever – and it won't until the very last moment of the case, ' he said to himself, as he sat on the driving seat of the caravan.

After around half an hour, they reached Hotel *Van Vihar.* It was a simple yet beautiful hotel situated in the lap of nature.

There was a short man at the gate waiting for them.

He greeted them as they dismounted the caravan. He went up to Robin and said happily, "Robin Bhaiyya, I am Tulsi, Somra Uncle's nephew. You haven't seen me, but I have seen your pictures."

Robin smiled and said, "It's nice meeting you, Tulsi. I hope you will show us good things in our trip to Palamu."

"Yes, Robin Bhaiyya, definitely," Tulsi said, as he escorted them inside. He asked the guard to get the caravan parked in the courtyard.

Babulalji walked beside Tulsi and asked him, "What are you doing at this hotel, Tulsi?"

Tulsi replied, "I sometimes work as a guide, Babulalji. There is a tourist from Kerala visiting this place. He is staying in this hotel. I am working as a guide for him."

"A tourist?" Robin asked, surprised.

"Yes, Dr. Verghese," he replied.

"Is that Dr. Stephen Verghese from Kerala?" Robin asked.

Tulsi thought for a minute and said, "Yes, Robin Bhaiyya. Why?"

Neil asked in a confused voice, "Who is Dr. Stephen Verghese?"

Robin smiled and said, "Either it is a very fortunate coincidence or a sign from above that this journey is going to be fruitful."

Babulalji whispered in Neil's ear, mimicking Robin, "There are no coincidences."

Chapter 33

Dr. Stephen Verghese was sitting in the canteen of the hotel on a white moulded plastic chair. He was reading a newspaper.

"Isn't it rather late for reading the newspaper, Dr. Verghese?" Robin asked.

Dr. Verghese looked at Robin in surprise and then again looked at the newspaper. There was a picture of Robin printed in the newspaper along with the news of the attack of the ghost on Professor Anil.

"Detective Horo, " Dr. Verghese said.

"You can call me, Robin," Robin replied.

By now, Babulalji, Neil and Naseem Bhai had reached there along with Tulsi. Robin introduced Dr. Verghese to them.

"This is Dr. Stephen Verghese, the famous historian and author of several books on the history of India."

He continued, "And right now, he is doing research for

his new book on the history of Jharkhand. Am I right, Dr. Verghese," Robin asked.

"Yes, you are right, Robin. But how do you know?" Dr. Verghese asked.

"I have your books in my library, Dr. Verghese, and I have read your last interview in the newspapers in which you had mentioned about your research for your new book that was going to be based on Jharkhand," Robin replied.

"Oh yes! You are right. I completely forgot about the interview," Dr. Verghese laughed.

He continued, "And Detective, my presence here right now is not a coincidence."

Babulalji and Neil looked at each other and smiled. They were used to hearing this phrase from Robin.

"So, what brings you here, Professor?" Robin asked.

Dr. Verghese looked him in the eye and said,

"The same thing that has brought you here, Detective, the Elixir of Doisa."

Chapter 34

Everyone including Robin was startled by what Dr. Verghese had just said.

"So, you know about the riddle?" Robin asked.

"Yes, I do, Detective, and I have seen the coins too," Dr. Verghese said.

They were taken aback. They did not know that someone else possessed the knowledge of the coins and the riddle.

"May I ask how do you know about it?" Robin asked.

"Because it was Professor Anand and I, who together discovered about the existence of this riddle and the coins." Replied Dr. Verghese

They were completely taken aback by this revelation. This was a game-changer, they thought. They were not alone in the quest of the 'Elixir of Doisa'. Someone else knew about it. At least someone who was still alive.

"Where did you find it, Dr. Verghese?" Robin asked.

Dr. Verghese smiled and replied, "Robin, in my opinion, the state of Jharkhand is heavily underestimated and ignored by historians and archaeologists. But it has a fascinating history associated with it. Have you ever visited the Shahpur Fort situated at Medininagar in Daltonganj?"

"No, I have not. Should I?" Robin asked.

Dr. Verghese looked at him and said, "Yes, you should. Everyone who has even a little bit of respect for history, should."

He then, added, "It was built by the Chero King, Gopal Ray during the years of the downfall of the Chero dynasty. After the attack of the British Army on the Palamu Fort, this was the place from where the Chero kings ruled in 1770 BC. The Shahpur Fort has a web of secret underground tunnels that lead even as far as the Palamu Fort and Rohtasgadh. These tunnels were used during the Mughal and British army attacks over Palamu Fort. There are many secret openings throughout this stretch that lead to God knows where."

He continued, "The irony is that many archaeologists and historians know about it. The opening of these tunnels can be seen easily in the Shahpur Fort, but nobody has ever bothered to explore them."

He looked around at the group who were listening spellbound.

He said: "But Professor Anand bothered to find out more about them. He was so sure about the legend of the Elixir of Doisa that he had heard about through the folklore of the region that he decided to go looking for it.

He wrote letters to me many times, until I decided to join him in this quest. We worked relentlessly day and night to find its location. We zeroed in on a part of those tunnels, but instead of the Elixir itself, we found a riddle and the ancient coins hidden inside the tunnel."

There was complete silence in the room. Everybody was engrossed in Dr. Verghese's story.

"Wow! That's an interesting story," Babulalji said.

Dr. Verghese looked at Robin and asked, "You do know what the Elixir of Doisa actually is, don't you?"

"Yes, we do. It's actually the name given to the treasure of Maharaja Medini Ray," Robin replied.

"You do know, but you do not understand, Robin. It could be the greatest and the biggest treasure the modern world has ever known! It could be the greatest find of this century," Dr. Verghese said in excitement with an expression in his eyes that almost bordered on madness.

He continued, "Professor Anand and I would have found it. We had solved most of the riddle. But since the last few weeks, he seemed very stressed. He was afraid of something. He had visited Palamu twice within the last two months since I met him. Something must have happened in those trips which he didn't tell me. I had decided to meet him in person, but he was killed before that. And that too by a ghost! But, then I decided I should continue this quest. The treasure needs to be found. History needs to give Raja Medini Ray his due credit as the great King he was. And that is why I am here, Robin."

Robin was listening to him with complete attention. He asked, "May I ask how much of the riddle have you solved?"

"That we will discuss later, Robin. You do have a plan to visit the Palamu Fort, don't you?" Dr. Verghese asked.

"Yes, we do," Robin replied.

"I will come along, too, Robin. But the fact that me and you both are here in this place means we are almost at the same point in solving the riddle. But there is one very important point in the riddle that needs to be addressed," Dr. Verghese said.

"What is that?" Robin asked.

"Who do you think is the 'knight' who protects the treasure?"

"Going by what has been happening, I think it is 'Satyabhama' who is protecting the treasure and killing anyone who has possession of the coins or the riddle," Robin replied.

"Yes, Robin, you are right. But even if we know he is the protector, the riddle does not give the location of the treasure. Don't you think that is so?" Dr. Verghese concluded.

"Yes, I do, but…." Robin was trying to say something, but Dr. Verghese interrupted him, "But it must mean that whoever this Satyabhama was, the treasure may be hidden at some place related to him. Most probably, his final resting place."

"Dr. Verghese, that's what I thought, too. But do you think a person by this name really existed in Raja Medini Ray's time? I couldn't find any proof of the existence of such a person in whatever books or documents I read about Palamu. And do you think that his ghost is still protecting the treasure even after three hundred and fifty years of his death?" Robin asked.

Dr. Verghese replied, "I don't know about the ghost, Robin. But as I told you earlier, Palamu is ignored by historians. That is why written historical accounts barely exist. Most of it is in the form of stories that the people of those times passed on to the next generation – history that became stories and after a few hundred years, was reduced to mere folklore and legends. But, I think, a person by this name did exist in Raja Medini Ray's time. Not in recorded history, but in so-called legends, he did exist."

The historian paused for a while to let this sink in. Then, he continued, "His name came up only after we found the coins and the riddle in the underground tunnels of the Shahpur Fort. Ranchi is not the only place which is haunted by the ghost of Satyabhama."

Robin was surprised. He asked, "Is it not?"

"No Robin. If we believe the rumours, the ghost of Satyabhama is haunting the Palamu Fort, too." Dr. Verghese replied.

"What?" It was evident that everybody in the room was startled.

Dr. Verghese leaned back on his chair and replied, "Yes, Robin. The hauntings started after we discovered the riddle and the coins. I don't believe in ghosts Robin, but rumours say this treasure is cursed. The riddle says that a knight protects the Elixir of Doisa. When we discovered the riddle that leads to the treasure, this knight, who we think is Satyabhama, rose from the dead to protect the treasure from us. I can't explain this; can you?"

Robin wanted to say something, but stopped. He asked, "What is the legend that you have heard about Satyabhama?"

Dr. Verghese smiled and said, "It's a fascinating story, Robin. A legend of unmatched and unthinkable loyalty. But I am not the narrator. Tulsi was taking me to an old man tonight who knows the stories of the kingdom of Maharaja Medini Ray. His ancestors worked in the court of the great King and passed on the stories down generations."

He continued, "It is late afternoon now. Soon darkness will cover the jungles. It is not safe to visit the Palamu Forts in the dark. Why don't we plan to visit the fort tomorrow early in the morning. Why don't you all accompany me today evening to hear the story of Satyabhama and the haunting of the Palamu Forts?"

"Where does this old man live?" Babulalji asked.

Tulsi replied, "He lives in Amwa village, Babulalji. It's near the Palamu Forts. My house is in Amwa, too. We can stay there for the night and then go to the fort early in the morning."

Robin looked at Naseem Bhai and Neil.

"What do you say, Naseem Bhai?" He asked.

"I think we should go. The night does fall early in the jungle. Besides, we too need to find who this Satyabhama is," Naseem Bhai replied.

Neil nodded in consent.

Babulalji said, "As long as I am away from the ghost, I am fine with wherever we go!"

Robin smiled and said, "Alright, then we will go to Amwa village with Dr. Verghese."

He continued, "This is the night when we will get to know the story of Satyabhama and the curse on the treasure."

Chapter 35

It was around 05:30 pm when they reached the village Amwa in Naseem Bhai's caravan. Dr. Verghese and Tulsi too had left their vehicle in hotel *Van Vihar* and travelled in the caravan with them.

Naseem Bhai parked the caravan in front of Tulsi's house. It was a small *pucca* house with three rooms and a little space in front of the house. The village had a mixture of the *pucca* houses and huts. There were many farms too where people could be seen working.

They freshened up and had some tea.

"We'll go to the old man's house at 07:00 pm. His grandson is my school friend. I have talked to him. He'll be there too."

It was dark when they reached the house of the old man. It was a relatively bigger house with a small 'hut' attached to it.

An old man was sitting on a wooden cot in front of the hut with a *'Hookah'*. There was a small fire lit in front of him in an earthen pot.

"Robin bhaiya, meet Mr. Guni Mahto. We call him '*daddu*' affectionately." Tulsi said.

Guni Mahto was a ninety years old man but he was still in his senses. He was wearing a light brown colored *khadi kurta* with white *dhoti*. He shook hands with Robin and said,

"I saw your picture in the newspaper."

Robin was pleasantly surprised by his good eye sight even at the age of ninety years.

"It's a pleasure meeting you Mr. Guni," Robin said.

Tulsi's friend and Guni's grandson Kamal came out of the house. He brought chairs for them. They all sat around the fire in front of Guni.

Kamal said, "*Daddu* used to work at 'Bihar secretariat' before Jharkhand came into existence. After his retirement he came back home and built this house. But he never demolished this hut. He repaired it and still lives in the hut only, while rest of the family lives in the *pucca* house."

"I was born in this hut and I want to die here too." Guni said.

Everyone was amazed by the fact that even at the age of ninety years, Guni was clear about his thoughts.

Kamal laughed and said, "You are not going to die anytime soon *daddu*!"

He continued, "*Daddu,* these people are here for the stories of Raja Medini Ray and Satyabhama."

"Yes I know. You told me earlier. I am not senile!" Guni replied.

Everybody couldn't help but laugh.

Dr. Verghese said, "Daddu I have studied every piece of recorded history of Palamu but couldn't find anybody by the name Satyabhama. I am told this name exists in some legends about the Palamu fort. Is it true? Was there someone named Satyabhama in the Times of Raja Medini Ray?"

Guni Mahto looked at him with his small eyes and said, "You have studied history but my ancestors who told me these stories had lived history. They had seen Raja Medini Ray and Satyabhama in flesh and bones. They had walked with them."

"Who was Satyabhama daddu? Tell us about him." Neil asked with curiosity.

Guni Mahto took a deep puff of *Hookah*. He looked at Neil and said, "If you want to know who he was, let me take you back in time."

Guni started narrating the story, "Satyabhama was a legend even in his own time. Nobody exactly knew where he came from. Some say he was an orphan whom Raja Medini Ray had brought from somewhere. Some say he was found in a temple as a baby and was a divine blessing of God to the King. But everybody knew that the King loved him like his own child and he loved him back like his own father.

He was an impenetrable shield and also the most terrifying and absolute weapon of Raja Medini Ray. No enemy, whether external or internal, could touch even the shadow of the King as long as Satyabhama was with him.

It is said once he fought a Tiger with his bare hands and saved the King's life in the jungles of Palamu.

He was the greatest warrior and strategist- kingdom of Palamu had ever seen. He was the head of the Royal guards of Raja Medini Ray but the King followed his advice in almost every matter, be it related to battle or to the development of Palamu. History is witness of the prosperity and growth of Palamu in the times of Raja Medini Ray, and Satyabhama played a very important part in it."

Guni Mahto took another puff of the *Hookah* and coughed out the smoke. Then he continued, "But there was something else that played a great part in it. It was an unimaginable treasure that Raja Medini Ray had won after defeating the King of Chhotanagpur.

But where there is prosperity and peace there are always some people who want to destroy it. The era of Raja Medini Ray was no exception.

Many corrupt ministers and officers in his court knew about the vastness of the treasure and wanted their share from it. They kept on plotting conspiracies against the King and his family. They wanted the Chero dynasty to fall so that they could have their share in the loot.

But Raja Medini Ray did not want the treasure which was meant for the people of Palamu, to fall in wrong hands.

So with the help of Satyabhama and his Royal guards he hid the treasure somewhere in his kingdom, the location of which was known only to a few of his trusted people.

The trail of the Treasure died but its legend lived on.

The traitors in the King's court kept looking for it and never stopped conspiring for it."

Guni Mahto had them spellbound by his story by now. He continued, "Then one day, Raja Medini Ray fell sick. On his death bed he asked Satyabhama to keep the treasure safe and disclose its location to his successor and Son Pratap Ray when the time was right and the traitors in his court were taken care of. But the time never came.

The great Raja Medini Ray died. Pratap Ray was given the throne of Palamu in the year 1674 AD.

After the death of Raja Medini Ray Satyabhama was devastated. The traitors thought of taking advantage of the turbulent time and plotted a conspiracy to assassinate Pratap Ray. They knew that Satyabhama, who was loyal to the throne and had now sworn to protect the new King, would come to his rescue.

A poisonous labyrinth was plotted.

On one fateful night when the new King Pratap Ray was resting in his chambers a handful of assassins dressed in black robes entered the King's palace.

Very silently they slit the throats of the Royal guards in the outer rim of the King's security.

But it was said that the Royal guards had loyalty and courage running in their veins. One of them hit the gong even with his dying breath.

The assassins were startled. They knew with the gong a storm will come. A storm named Satyabhama. A storm they did not want to face.

Satyabhama was resting in his quarters when he heard the gong. Within a few seconds he came out and mounted his black stallion.

The stallion ran like a wild thunder."

Everyone was on the edge of their seat now. Guni Mahto continued, "Back in the palace two of the assassins had reached the King who was alone in his corridor. One of them lifted his sword to attack the King. Pratap Ray took out his sword to counter the attack.

But just in that moment two arrows flew in air simultaneously like the bolts of lightning. One of the arrows pierced the sword carrying hand of the assassin and stuck it to the adjacent wall. The other one pierced his throat!

Pratap Ray looked down from the corridor in amazement. He knew only one archer in his kingdom who could do this.

Satyabhama had arrived.

The assassins had not expected him to come so soon. They abandoned their mission of assassinating the King and tried to escape.

But death himself had come for them in the form of Satyabhama. His sword was deadly and unstoppable. In a matter of minutes he had killed most of the assassins.

But the two of them who were on the far end of the palace managed to escape on their horses.

Satyabhama saw that the rest of the Royal guards had arrived and the King was safe. The forces patrolling the walls of the fort had also come. He decided to follow the escaping assassins. He wanted to catch them alive and reach the mastermind behind this assassination attempt. A few of his soldiers of Royal guards followed him.

But Satybhama didn't know it was not a plan to assassinate the King. It was a plan to bring him out of the Fort alone. His soldiers were attacked by the traitors from both sides a few meters from the fort and were killed. Satyabhama who was not aware of their fate followed the assassins into the dense jungle.

He had walked into the trap."

Guni Mahto paused and looked at his audience as a to palpate their tension. He then continued, "As soon as he entered the jungle he was surrounded by enemies which numbered at least an odd fifty. They knew it was the finest warrior of the kingdom they wanted to catch and they were afraid of his legend. They did not want to take any chance with him.

Satyabhama looked at them and recognised one of them who was sitting atop a white horse with his face covered with a black mask.

"Santosh Singh. I can see through your mask, you traitor."Satyabhama shouted.

Santosh Singh was the finance minister of the kingdom

of Palamu. He was startled at first but then he removed his mask and said,

"Satyabhama I know you are Loyal to the King and I really respect that. But please think rationally. You yourself know that the treasure hidden by your late King is priceless. I promise you if you lead me to the treasure I will give you one fifth part of it.

Don't act recklessly Satyabhama. Join hands with me. We could be rich. Besides, the King Medini Ray is dead. Why do you want to give your life for the promise of a dead King? My men can kill you easily if you don't cooperate with me. You are outnumbered."

Satyabhama looked straight into his eyes and drew his sword slowly. He said, "Do you see fear in my eyes? I see it in yours and your men's eyes."

With these words the greatest warrior of Palamu fought the enemies alone. His sword tore through the army of traitors. He had killed almost half of the assassins, but they couldn't draw even a drop of his blood. He was painting the landscape red with his deadly sword. Santosh Singh was awestruck by his bravery and skills. His heart filled with respect for him. But he was enemy and they needed to catch him by all means possible. He knew his men were no match for him.

Not in a fair fight.

Santosh Singh signaled his archers who were hiding in the jungle.

A few arrows flew from a distance and pierced Satyabhama's chest from behind. He was brought down on his knees.

He was captured and taken in the deep forest bound in chains. He was tortured but he didn't disclose the secret place where the treasure was hidden. They even smeared his arms with oil and put them on fire but they could not break him.

They were running out of time. Suddenly they heard the shouts of King's soldiers in the distance. Commander Trishul Singh was coming for him. Santosh Singh looked at Satyabhama. He was not going to survive. He left him there and fled."

Guni Mahto paused and took another deep puff on the *Hookah*. His audience was getting restless. They did not want him to stop. So, he continued, "With great difficulty Satyabhama managed to get hold of a bow and an arrow from the body of a dead assassin lying in front of him. Because of the fire on his arms the arrow caught fire too as it was lying in the pool of the flammable oil. He sat and positioned himself with his back against the trunk of a tree. He aimed the arrow towards the fleeing Santosh Singh. His arms were shaking. His vision was blurring. But he wanted to make that shot so that the man conspiring against his dead King's legacy gets punished.

He wanted to shoot an arrow one last time.

The burning arrow flew scorching the air surrounding it.

Santosh Singh felt a jolt on the left side of his chest. He looked down. He saw an arrow had pierced his chest from behind.

Satyabhama saw him falling off his horse in a distance. He smiled.

Just in that moment Trishul Singh reached the place along with the soldiers.

He was devastated to see Satyabhama sitting against a tree in severely wounded condition. He ordered some soldiers to follow the fleeing traitors. He sat beside Satyabhama holding him in his arms.

"What have they done?" Trishul Singh cried.

Satyabhama opened his eyes and consoled him.

"Don't…. Don't cry Trishul Singh. I got him with my arrow. It was…it was Santosh Singh. He wanted the location of *baba's* treasure…He tortured me but I didn't tell him. I could have killed them all…but... but they attacked me from behind…cowards."

It was a secret between him and Trishul Singh. Satyabhama never had the courage to address his King as '*baba*' but whenever he and Trishul Singh were alone he would address Raja Medini Ray as '*baba*', as he always saw his father in him.

Trishul Singh could not hold back his tears hearing Satyabhama addressing his dead King as '*baba*'.

It seemed even God could not.

For the sky was torn by the sound of a loud thunder. It started raining.

The great warrior with a body made of stone now seemed like a small vulnerable kid talking to him about his father. And then he fell silent."

Guni Mahto paused again and looked at his speechless audience. They had an expression of sadness on their faces. He then continued, "Trishul Singh held the lifeless body of Satyabhama in his arms and cried for god knows how long. His soldiers stood surrounding him. Because of the rain one could not make out whether they were crying or not.

But they must have.

For their Hero and the greatest of the warriors their kingdom had ever seen was dead.

The sixteen years old thin orphan village boy who gave the last of his food to his King was dead."

Chapter 36

1674 AD
Palamu, Jharkhand

Trishul Singh wiped his tears and stood up keeping Satyabhama's lifeless body against the tree.

He addressed the soldiers of Royal guards.

"We don't know whom we can trust in the palace. Satyabhama gave his life protecting the King's treasure. His sacrifice must not go in vain. The treasure must not fall into wrong hands."

He took out a small red colored velvet pouch from under his armour and handed it over to one of the loyal soldiers of the Royal guards 'Abhijit Mahto'.

Then he said, "I am going to '*Gaya*' to warn Satyabhama's sister Meera about the traitors. Her life could be in danger too. She is my responsibility now. If I do not return give this pouch to the King. It contains the location of the treasure. Protect it with your life. It is for the hands of Raja Pratap Ray and no one else."

He took out six gold coins embossed with the face of late Raja Medini Ray and gave it to him.

"Give them to the King. He'll know it is true and not some conspiracy."

Trishul Singh said and kept the lifeless body of Satyabhama on his horse and galloped away in the dark stormy night.

Nobody saw Commander Trishul Singh again. Nobody knew what happened to him. Was he killed by the traitors on his way to Gaya? Did he reach Gaya to warn Meera? What happened to Satyabhama's body?

There were only cold relentless questions but no answers.

The soldier Abhijit Mahto delivered the red pouch and five gold coins to the King. In the pouch there was the location of the treasure in the form of a riddle, embossed on a piece of leather, which nobody could solve.

Two of the greatest warriors of Palamu, commander Trishul Singh and Satyabhama were gone.

The great treasure was lost in the indifferent and unforgiving womb of time.

Only a weak trail lingered in the form of a riddle. It waited for someone to come and solve it. Maybe even after a few centuries.

Chapter 37

There was an absolute silence in front of Guni Mahto's hut. They were still looking at the old man in awe who had just completed the amazing story of Satyabhama and was taking a deep puff of the *Hookah.*

Somehow they were feeling sad about Styabhama's death. They had developed a strange respect for him in their hearts after hearing his story.

The old man puffed out the smoke and said. "Nobody knew what happened to the body of Satyabhma. It was gone. Some say he was given as a gift by God to Raja Medini Ray and he took him back after his death.

It was said he cursed the treasure that if anybody other than a member of the royal family tried to find the treasure his ghost would haunt him and kill him.

The treasure was lost too. Nobody could find it. Soon the Chero dynasty withered and faded and Palamu was brought under the British rule.

After years and years of fruitless search the stories of that unimaginable treasure were reduced to mere fairy tales and rumors. People stopped believing in it.

But it seems someone has again started looking for it, for the ghost of Satyabhama has risen again from the dead and he is roaming in the Palamu fort."

"His ghost is haunting the Palamu fort?" Naseem Bhai asked in surprise. Babulalji was frightened. Robin had again brought him near the ghost of Satyabhama.

Guni Mahto again took a deep puff of *Hookah* and said, "Yes he is haunting the Palamu forts. This started on a night of full moon last month.

Two thieves of our neighbouring village had looted a few houses in our village. When the villagers followed them they took refuge in the Palamu fort. They hid in the passageway built in the walls of the fort. But there they had a frightening encounter with the ghost. They said the lamps in the walls of the passageway burst in fire spontaneously and the ghost of Satyabhama appeared out of a white mist. They ran for their life and encountered the villagers who were looking for them.

They got beaten badly by the villagers but they were happy that at least they were not killed by the ghost.

Since then there were many sightings of the ghost of Satyabhama in the ruins of the fort at night. People heard many strange voices coming out of the fort. Nobody used to go to the area of the fort in the night but after the haunting started people avoided going there in day time also."

Robin was in deep thoughts. Dr. Verghese was looking at him.

Tulsi tried to lighten the atmosphere and said, "Of course these are mere stories. How can we believe in ghosts?"

Guni Mahto looked at him and said to Robin, "I don't know where this generation is going."

They could not help but laugh.

The old man rose up from his cot and walked inside the hut with the help of his stick. They were a little confused about what he was doing. He came out after a good five minutes. He had something in his hand. He kept it on Robin's palm.

It was dark but Robin recognized it.

"What is it Dada?" Neil asked.

Robin lowered his palm near the fire. It was a gold coin. It was relatively old and frayed but they recognized it immediately.

It had a face of a King embossed on one side and on the other side there was a small scripture in Devnagri script.

"*To Raja Medini Ray with love.*"

Everyone present there was surprised.

"How did you get this?" Dr. Verghese asked.

Guni Mahto replied, "My great great great grandfather was in the Royal guards of Raja Medini Ray. It was given to him by a commander of the King's army to deliver to the King. There were six of them but he had kept one with him and had delivered the rest to the King. Not because he wanted to steal it, but because he wanted to keep it as a souvenir of his Great King."

Robin gave it back to him and asked for his permission to leave.

The old man shook his hand and said, "If you solve this case I would give this coin to you."

Robin smiled and thanked him for his generosity.

They left Guni Mahto's house and walked towards the house of Tulsi. The night was lit by the dim bluish light of the gibbous moon and occasional lamp posts on the *kaccha* roads of the village.

"Dada this explains why there is fire everywhere when the Ghost of Satyabhama arrives and also why the ghost's arms are ablaze with fire. Because he died like that." Neil said.

"Yes Neil it seems so." Robin replied.

"Robin after hearing the story of Satyabhama, even I am convinced that it is a real ghost. I mean every part of his story checks out. Be it the gold coins, the riddle or the history associated with it. Don't you think so?" Naseem Bhai asked.

"I think it's a little bit too perfect." Robin replied without looking at him.

Dr. Verghese who was walking besides Robin said,

"This story does confirm that in the riddle the knight who protects the treasure is Satyabhama indeed. But it still doesn't tell us about his last resting place or where the treasure could be hidden."

Robin said, "Yes you are right Dr. Verghese but at least we got to know his story. And I believe after our visit to the Palamu fort tomorrow we would get answers to some more questions."

"Amen." Naseem Bhai said.

They reached Tulsi's home and had a nice dinner. They requested Tulsi to put their beds on the terrace as they wanted to sleep beneath the starry sky. Dr. Verghese was not keen on sleeping on terrace as he had some study to complete before sleeping. Tulsi made comfortable beds for them on the terrace and lit two mosquito coils on both sides of the terrace. But Babulalji was not satisfied with it and applied mosquito repellent cream over his body.

They all were tired from the journey and they had to start early in the morning for the Palamu fort so they went to sleep.

At around 03:00 am a shadow stood beneath a tree few meters from Tulsi's house. He had an oil-lamp in his hands. He swung the lamp twice and signalled someone.

A few minutes later another mysterious shadow came out of Tulsi's house. He looked around to make sure nobody was watching him and then slowly moved towards the tree.

The two of them had a small conversation and the

shadow with the lamp went away. A minute later the other shadow too came back to Tulsi's house.

The wheels of conspiracies were spinning in full swing. Just like they once had three hundred and fifty years ago in the kingdom of Palamu.

The cursed treasure was once protected at the cost of Satyabhama's blood. Whose blood was it going to be this time?

Chapter 38

In the village, the day starts early. Neil was woken up by the crowing of a rooster. He looked around. Robin and Naseem Bhai were not there. Babulalji was still snoring. He saw Robin and Naseem Bhai were already down and were talking in front of the caravan.

He shook Babulalji awake.

"Babulalji, wake up. It's 6:30 in the morning."

"Where are Horo Babu and Naseem Bhai?" he asked.

"They are already down there," Neil said, pointing towards the caravan.

"All right. Let's go down."

In the meantime, Tulsi came up on the terrace with tea.

"You are awake. Robin Bhaiyya asked me to wake you up."

Neil and Babulalji took a sip from their hot steaming cup of tea.

"There is a water well behind our house if you want to take a bath," Tulsi said with a smile.

Neil and Babulalji looked at each other and shrugged.

A few minutes later, they came out after freshening up. Dr. Verghese had come out too by that time.

"Are we going to start early for the fort?" he asked.

"Yes, Dr. Verghese, we are all set," Naseem Bhai replied.

It was 7:30 am by the time they started for the Palamu Fort in the caravan.

Naseem Bhai was driving and Robin and Neil were sitting next to him. Babulalji, Dr. Verghese and Tulsi were seated in the back.

They entered the road that led inside the forest area. There were many langoors up in the trees.

Neil noticed that the grass and bushes had been cleared very neatly upto a few meters from both sides of the road.

"Who has done this, Tulsi Bhaiyya?" he asked.

"Some local people and workers from the forest department clear the grass and bushes from either side of the road to prevent forest fires. Sometimes, travellers or passersby carelessly throw burning cigarette butts on the side of the road where the dry grass and bushes can catch fire and lead to a forest fire." Tulsi replied.

"Wow! That's very thoughtful of them," Neil said.

After a few minutes' drive, Babulalji looked decidedly restless.

"How far is it?" he asked.

"You will see it soon, Babulalji. Just keep looking ahead," replied Tulsi.

And then they saw it.

From among the trees, the fort was visible atop a small hill. They could now see the enormous outer wall and the watchtower of the fort.

"Whoa! It's enormous and beautiful! It reminds me of the Jaisalmer Fort," Babulalji said.

"There are two forts here, Babulalji. The old fort and the new fort. The one you are seeing right now is the old fort," Tulsi said.

After driving for a few meters more, they reached the new fort. It was built around the slopes of a hill that was conical in shape. There were two rows of walls that had been built in the shape of a perfect square. The outer wall was thick with passages along the roof between the battlements. The walls had galleries that opened out into the interior of the fort. They were awestruck by its sheer beauty and enormity.

"This fort really deserves more attention. It's so beautiful that it's painful to see it in ruins. I have seen the Jaisalmer Fort and I don't think this fort is anything less than that one. It just needs some renovation and taking care of," Naseem Bhai said.

They saw the ruins of an old mosque outside the fort. They left the caravan and reached the fabled Nagpuri gate of the new fort. It was huge and stunning. Beautiful carvings and patches of Meenakari could still be seen on the gate.

"It's really beautiful," Neil said.

"Yes, it is. But Raja Medini Ray had got this Nagpuri gate bricked up because he thought the side of the wall on which it was set was unlucky. But later, it was opened again by the government," Tulsi said.

They crossed the astonishingly beautiful Nagpuri gate and entered a circular room just within the gate where there was a water-well.

"The well was dug to provide a supply of drinking water to the soldiers in case of a siege on the fort," Tulsi said. They looked down the well. It was dry and silted up. They now entered the main courtyard towards the right side of the gate. There was a passageway built inside the thick wall of the fort. Babulalji and Neil went near its opening and peeped inside.

"Wow! Horo Babu these passageways are built inside the walls. They must have been used by soldiers during patrolling or during battles," Babulalji said.

"Yes, Babulalji, you are right," Tulsi replied.

Naseem Bhai looked inside and said, "Robin, we should take a look inside. It could be the same passageway where the thieves from Guni Mahto's story must have hid."

He entered the passageway and saw the old rusty torches on the wall. The adjoining portions of the wall were stained black with soot.

"The torches were lit recently. This is definitely the same passageway, Robin," he announced, while putting his hand inside one of the torches.

"There is ash inside it, too," Naseem Bhai said.

Robin, who was still standing outside, said without looking at him, "Reddish-coloured ash?"

Naseem Bhai looked at the ash in his hand and was surprised. "Yes, reddish-coloured ash! But how did you know? You haven't seen it!"

Robin spoke again without looking at him, "And the torches have a hole in their bottoms?"

Naseem Bhai looked at the bottom of the torches. He was startled. "Yes, they have small holes! But…but how do you know?"

They all were amazed. How did Robin know all this?

Babulalji said, "Horo Babu, please tell me, do you have some superpowers? How did you know all this?"

Robin laughed and said, "No, Babulalji. I don't have any superpowers. And don't worry, you will get to know everything soon."

But Babulalji was not satisfied with this answer. He looked at Neil, who looked equally confused. Dr. Verghese was looking at Robin with a straight face. He appeared to be admiring his powers of observation.

They moved ahead and saw another small mosque inside the main courtyard.

"This mosque was not here, initially. It was built after the conquest of the Palamu Forts by the Mughal commander Daud Khan in 1660. It was a fierce battle. Dr. Verghese is the person who can tell us more about this conquest," Tulsi said looking at Dr. Verghese.

"Yes, Dr. Verghese, please do tell us something about that battle," Babulalji insisted.

They were all now looking at him. He seemed reluctant, but then agreed. He began, "The year was 1660. The Mughal general Daud Khan left Patna with a strong force to conquer Palamu. The kingdom of the Chero kings now extended upto South Gaya. To reach the Palamu Fort, Daud Khan needed to conquer three outer frontier forts of the Chero kings. The first one was Kothi, located six miles south of Imamganj to the south of Gaya district. He conquered it and marched ahead. His next target was the second fort, Kunda, a hilly fort that took the large army of Daud Khan more than a month to reach as it was surrounded by dense forests and wild animals.

His army painstakingly cleared a path through the jungles so that there was a road to move ahead. He conquered the second fort, too, and was now planning to reach the third fort, following the same strategy of clearing the jungles and establishing a road to reach the third fort 'Devgan' and raze it to the ground.

On December 9, 1660, Daud Khan had reached within two miles of Palamu city. The Cheros had fortified their army and were ready for the inevitable battle. Seeing their preparations, Daud Khan tried to buy time and tried negotiating with the Chero King. He offered the King the title of emperor that specified that the Chero King had embraced Islam and offered his state as a tribute to the Mughal emperor.

But even before he could get a reply from the Chero King, one of his contingents of soldiers launched an attack on the Cheros. Daud Khan had no choice but to jump into the fray. The Cheros were surprised by this attack and had to retreat. But during the night, they brought two large canons from the fort and mounted them on their bastions and attacked Daud Khan's army.

But Daud Khan was determined to win this battle. His army dragged their guns to a hill that overlooked the bastions and bombarded them. The Cheros retreated to the lower fort. But Daud Khan's soldiers crossed the river and attacked the town at the foot of the lower fort. The battle continued and the Chero kings had to retreat to the upper fort where the King continued to fight for some time after sending his family and valuables into hiding in the jungles. But the Cheros who were depleted of both manpower and material could not continue the fight for long and fled to the jungles.

And so the Palamu Fort was captured by Daud Khan's army and the whole region of Palamu came under Mughal rule.

It is believed these invasions took place during the reign of Anant Ray while his relative Pratap Ray fought against the army of Daud Khan," Dr. Verghese concluded.

They were mesmerized by the story. It seemed they had stepped back in time and could feel a part of the upheaval that had happened so many years ago. Listening to the story inside the very fort where it all happened was an experience beyond description. They could hear the shouts and battle cries of the soldiers and the sounds of the canons. They saw history unfolding itself in front of their eyes.

Marks of canons and bullets could still be seen on the walls of the fort which had been inflicted upon them during the countless battles they had witnessed. But the great Palamu Fort was still standing with all its might, much like a silent witness of innumerable victories and losses that had been staged within its walls.

After a few minutes of silence, Naseem Bhai asked, "So, Dr. Verghese these two relatives, Anant Ray and Pratap Ray are supposed to be the 'two friends' mentioned in the riddle?"

"Yes, it appears so," Dr. Verghese replied.

"But Raja Medini Ray was crowned King after them. His battle with the King of Chhotanagpur in which he won the treasure also dates after the period of Anant Ray and Pratap Ray. Then why are these two mentioned in the riddle," Naseem Bhai questioned.

"Yes, indeed, Dr. Verghese. That is what I was thinking, too. Somehow it doesn't sound logical. What do you think, Horo Babu?" Babulalji asked turning towards Robin.

Robin was looking away with his back towards them. Everyone's attention was drawn to him. He was looking at the enormous and timeless walls of the Palamu Fort.

He said in a calm voice,

"Babulalji, we have got it all wrong."

Chapter 39

"What do you mean, Robin? What have we got wrong," Dr. Verghese asked, sounding a bit desperate.

"Everything, Dr. Verghese. Other than the first line of the riddle, we have got it all wrong!" Robin replied.

"Oh my God! Horo Babu does it mean you have solved the puzzle?" Babulalji asked in excitement.

"Yes, Babulalji, I have," Robin replied in a matter-of-fact voice.

Babulalji was excited.

"I knew Horo Babu you would solve it! I never doubted you. I knew if there is anyone in this whole world who could solve this three hundred and fifty-year-old riddle, it's you!"

"Do you…do you really know the location where the treasure is hidden, Robin?" Dr. Verghese asked in amazement.

"Yes, I do," Robin replied, looking at him.

Dr. Verghese could not believe his ears.

"Do you know what you are saying? Oh God, I can't believe it! He did it! They were right! Detective Horo found the treasure!"

Neil seemed to be in utter shock.

Naseem Bhai looked at Robin. He recalled something Robin had told him near the caravan in the morning.

"Tell us, Horo Babu what does the puzzle mean? Where is the priceless treasure of Raja Medini Ray hidden?" Babulalji asked.

"Babulalji, patience. I will tell you," he replied.

Everyone's attention was focused completely on Robin now. They didn't want to miss even a single word said by him.

He continued, "The first line of the puzzle is

'Where there is death among the trees due to frost'

This line does indicate that the treasure is hidden somewhere in Palamu. As I explained earlier, some people believe that the name 'Palamu' was derived from *Pala* meaning frost and *mu* meaning dead.

Now we come to the second line,

'Near the sharp fangs of Ornaga, it lies lost'

'Ornaga' is not a statue with fangs!"

Dr. Verghese interrupted, "Then what is it?"

Robin continued, "Ornaga is another name of the *Auranga* River that flows near the Palamu Fort. It is said that the river bank looks like a set of jagged teeth due to extensive rock exposures in the bed of the river which look like sharp fangs. That means the treasure is lost somewhere near the *Auranga* river."

They were shocked by this revelation and were admiring Robin's 'sharper-than-laser' brains.

"I realized this when we stopped at *Kechki* yesterday while coming to Palamu. *Kechki* is the confluence of the North *Koel* River and *Auranga* or *Ornaga* River," Robin continued.

Then he said again, "Now coming to the next lines,

Three resolute warriors guard the two friends,
Who are tormented by battles, some won some lost.'

The man who wrote this riddle was never talking about Anant Ray and Pratap Ray. These two names were never meant to indicate the location of the treasure. He was talking about the two friends who had been tormented by multiple battles and had witnessed many victories and losses too. He was talking about the Palamu Forts itself! The two friends in the riddle are none other than the old and the new Palamu Forts!"

Neil asked, "But who are the 'Three resolute warriors', Dada?"

Robin continued, "The three resolute warriors in the riddle are none other than the three outer frontier forts of Palamu -- Kothi, Kunda and Devgan, which Daud Khan had to conquer before attacking the Palamu Forts. These 'three' frontier forts always guarded the 'two' Palamu Forts from their enemies."

Dr. Verghese was awestruck. "Only you could deduce this, Robin. I am your diehard fan now. You are a genius."

Naseem Bhai said in excitement, "But Robin that means the treasure is hidden right here somewhere in between these two old and new forts!"

Robin replied, "Yes, Naseem Bhai. The unimaginable treasure of Raja Medini Ray is hidden in these forts!"

"Oh my God! The treasure is right here somewhere beneath our feet!" Babulalji was ecstatic.

Dr. Verghese held Robin's shoulders in excitement. "But where, Robin? Where in these forts? Is Satyabhama's body buried in the fort itself? Where is his last resting place?"

But Robin was distracted now. He walked a few steps and squatted on the ground. He was looking at something very carefully. He touched something on the ground. They were not sure what he was looking at.

"Have some patience, Dr. Verghese. I know where exactly the treasure is hidden in these forts. But before I tell you that, we need to leave this place immediately." Robin said.

"But…but why? If the treasure is here, why are we going back?" Dr. Verghese asked Robin.

"Yes, Horo Babu, why are we going back? Let's see where it is hidden!" Babulalji said, sounding brave.

Robin was still examining something on the ground. He turned back, still squatting, and gestured them to keep quiet.

"Don't make any sound," he said.

"I think a tiger is around!"

Chapter 40

"A tiger? What are you saying? How could a tiger possibly be here?" Babulalji asked.

"Babulalji, if there is ever a possibility of seeing a tiger in Jharkhand, It is right here. The Palamu Forts come under the Betla National Park area, which is home to tigers. And trust me, the King of jungle is around," Robin said, pointing at the fresh pug marks of a tiger on the ground.

They crowded around the place where Robin was squatting and saw the marks.

"How can you say these are a tiger's pug marks?" Dr. Verghese asked.

"The mark has four toes and a three-lobed pad. It is a tiger's pug mark for sure," Robin replied.

"Don't tigers have five toes?" Dr. Verghese asked again.

"Yes, they do. The fifth one is called 'dewclaw'. But ordinarily, it doesn't touch the ground and hence is not seen in the pug marks, as the fifth claw is retractable and is a part of a tiger's weaponry." Robin explained.

Babulalji was frightened. He said, "First, a ghost and now a tiger! Horo Babu you will definitely get me killed this time."

Robin asked him to calm down and said, "Don't panic, Babulalji. Let's get out of here very quietly without making any noise."

They came out of the fort huddled together. They were alert and looking out for the tiger in every direction. Robin had his pistol with him, but he was praying he doesn't have to use it.

They saw their caravan parked a few meters away from the gate of the fort.

"There it is. Let's run for the caravan," Babulalji said in a trembling voice.

Robin stopped him and whispered, "We won't make it."

He pointed his finger towards his right. Everybody followed the direction of his finger. At a distance of barely a few meters, sat a fearsome but magnificent tiger among the trees. His back was towards them and his skin was shining like wild fire in the sunlight.

"Oh God! what do we do? What do we do?" Babulalji was shuddering like a leaf in a storm.

Naseem Bhai gestured to him to keep quiet and said, "We'll slowly move towards the caravan. He is not paying attention to us. Perhaps, he is not hungry. I will count to three and then we start moving."

"One…" he said.

At the count of one only, Babulalji ran towards the caravan and closed its door after entering it! The tiger heard the sound of the closing of the door and turned his head towards them. Robin and Naseem Bhai looked at each other. Robin held Neil's hand and said, "Run!"

They ran towards the caravan. The tiger did too. The tiger was a little farther away from the caravan comparatively, but he was much faster.

They had to outrun a certain death. Robin was dragging Neil with him, who in turn was looking at the tiger running like a lightning bolt. He could see his dagger-like teeth very close to him now. The tiger jumped and lifted his claw in readiness for the kill. Neil closed his eyes. 'This is the end,' he thought.

Then he heard a loud 'thud'. Robin had pulled him inside the caravan and closed the door. There had been a difference of only a fraction of a second between the closing of the door and the tiger striking a thunderous blow of his paw on the door of caravan, leaving a deep scratch with his four deadly.

They couldn't believe they had outrun the tiger. Their hearts were racing like wild horses. They looked at each other to make sure everyone was on board.

"I said I would count to three! You ran at one!" Naseem Bhai said looking at Babulalji.

"I am sorry! I panicked!" Babulalji replied. He was still trying to control his labored breathing.

However, there was only one problem. They all, including Naseem Bhai, had climbed into the backseat. Naseem Bhai and Robin now slowly moved towards the front seat.

Meanwhile, the tiger was frustrated. He was circling the caravan smelling his prey. Babulalji was looking at him with one eye closed and reciting *Hanuman Chalisa*. Neil, Dr. Verghese and Tulsi were still trying to regain their breath.

The tiger stopped circling the caravan and stood just in front of the door where Babulalji was seated. Babulalji could see the vapours on the glass of his window caused by the tiger's hot breath. With a swift leap, he stood up on his hind limbs and placed the weight of his fore limbs on the handle of the door.

With a 'click' the door opened!

Babulalji screamed. Naseem Bhai quickly pulled the door back and locked it from inside!

"Babulalji, why didn't you lock the door from inside?" he shouted.

"I didn't know tigers can open doors!" he replied, trembling.

Naseem Bhai had by now reached the driving seat. Robin too sat beside him. He started the caravan and they drove away from the fort. The King of the jungle watched the caravan going away but didn't make any effort to follow it.

Naseem Bhai looked into the rearview mirror. The tiger leapt back into the trees and disappeared from view.

They travelled in complete silence for a few minutes, and then Naseem Bhai laughed.

Robin looked at him and smiled.

"My God! That was something! I am never going to repair the door of my caravan where the tiger hit it. It will always be a reminder of our adventure, Robin!" Naseem Bhai said reassuringly, "Don't be afraid, guys. We outran a tiger! We should be happy!"

They smiled. It was an experience they were never likely to forget.

They drove for another half-hour and then stopped in front of a roadside *dhaba*.

There were a few vehicles parked outside it. They sat on the wooden benches outside the *dhaba*.

Dr. Verghese said, "I'll go ask them for some tea." He went inside.

There were a few people sitting on the benches outside. Robin looked at Naseem Bhai. He stood and went to attend nature's call and came back after a few minutes.

Dr. Verghese had returned with a glass of tea in his hand. The waiter brought tea for them in small glasses. They sat together, sipping a much-needed glass of tea.

"Robin, can you now tell us where the treasure is hidden in the fort? Where is the last resting place of Satyabhama?" Dr. Verghese asked in an urgent, but low voice.

"Dr. Verghese, I think we should talk to Inspector Patrick first. I think we are being followed here too," Robin said.

"Followed? By whom?" Dr. Verghese asked.

There was less sugar in the tea. Robin took another sip and asked the waiter for a spoon of sugar and continued, "A mysterious gang is following us. Its members have a particular 'hawk tattoo' on their wrists. I think it is a gang led by a criminal named 'Buru'. Can you see the man sitting on the bench right behind us?" Robin asked.

Dr. Verghese and the others too looked towards him.

Robin continued, "He is in disguise here, but he is the same man I had chased near the police station a couple of days ago."

They were both surprised and afraid at the same time. Meanwhile the waiter came with a spoon of sugar and put it in Robin's tea. Robin's eyes drifted towards his wrist. There was a 'hawk' tattoo on his wrist.

'Oh no! I have made a mistake! How could I be such a fool!' Robin thought. But it was too late. His head was spinning. He saw Babulalji, Neil, Naseem Bhai, Tulsi and Dr. Verghese, who had all finished their tea, drop down to the ground.

He realized that everyone in the *dhaba* at that time was a member of the mysterious gang. They must have captured the staff of the *dhaba* and were waiting for them to come.

He had walked right into their trap.

Robin was struggling to stand straight. His head was spinning like a top.

A man came forward and helped him stand. "We finally meet, Detective Horo."

Robin couldn't see him because of his blurred vision. But he knew who he was. "Buru…?" he asked.

The man laughed and said, "You are really a genius!"

Someone landed a sharp blow on Robin's head from behind and his head spun in darkness.

Once more, the cursed treasure of Palamu was asking for its share of blood.

Chapter 41

Robin regained consciousness slowly. His blurred vision was now getting better. He had a throbbing pain in his head. He realized he was lying on the grass. He lifted his head and looked around and saw the enormous walls of the Palamu Fort again.

'Are we back in the fort? he wondered. It was the large courtyard of the new fort. And immediately, he was worried about Neil, Babulalji, Tulsi and Naseem Bhai.

'Where are they?' he thought and reached for the pistol in his pocket. It was not there.

A voice came from behind him. "The genius Detective Horo is awake."

Robin recognized the voice. It was the same voice he had heard before he had lost consciousness. He got up on his feet and turned back. Before him stood a middle-aged man of almost the same height as him. The man had a muscular build and was wearing a brown biker's jacket over his black T shirt and blue jeans. Behind him stood his men including the one Robin had chased near the *Harmu* Police Station.

"You are the infamous gangster, Buru?" Robin asked.

"Guilty as charged," the man said.

"Where are my friends?" Robin asked.

"Don't worry, I haven't killed them yet. But I will soon," Buru replied and asked his men to bring them out.

Buru's men brought Babulalji, Neil, Naseem Bhai, Tulsi and Dr. Verghese from the old mosque in the fort at gunpoint.

"I must warn you, it's not safe here. There was a tiger here just a few hours earlier," Babulalji said in a shaky voice.

The man asked him to shut up and pointed his gun towards the left side of the mosque. The dead body of the tiger was lying in the corner.

"You killed him! Monsters!" Babulalji said in anger.

Robin was relieved to see they were unhurt. He looked at them. They looked frightened.

Buru asked his men to bring Dr. Verghese forward and kept the gun over his head. "Robin you know why we are here. So, let's avoid beating around the bush and come to the point. Where is the treasure hidden in this fort? I don't think an intelligent person like you needs to be told that if you don't tell me, I'll start shooting people, starting with this one," he said, pointing his gun towards Dr. Verghese.

Dr. Verghese was almost on the verge of crying. He closed his eyes. Robin looked straight at Buru and said calmly, "Me and you both know that you are not going to shoot him. So why don't 'you' stop beating around the bush?"

Buru smiled and said, "I really love this boy!"

He removed his gun from Dr. Verghese's head and said, "I told you, Dr. Verghese he will solve the puzzle, but he'll see right through you. He will know you are involved in this from the minute he sees you!"

Dr. Verghese shrugged his shoulders and said, "Yes, you did Buru. But it was a risk we needed to take. And see, it has paid off. He has solved that three hundred and fifty-year-old riddle."

Babulalji and Neil were surprised to learn that Dr. Verghese was involved in this conspiracy!

Buru now pointed his gun towards Naseem Bhai, "Now we come to the question again. Where is the treasure hidden, Detective?"

Robin replied, angry now: "Don't point the gun at my friends. You'll regret this once you are without that gun in your hand."

Buru promptly kept the gun in his pocket and said, "Very well. Let's see what you can do. I don't have the gun in my hand now."

Babulalji and Neil were excited. They knew Buru can't win in a hand-to-hand combat with Robin. Nobody can.

Buru attacked Robin with a right hook. Robin blocked it deftly with his left arm and then the unthinkable happened.

With unbelievable speed, Buru landed another punch on Robin's face with his other hand. Robin fell on the ground. He jumped up and tried to land a punch on Buru's face, but he just leaned back and planted a thunderous round kick on Robin's face. Robin was again back on the ground. Robin tasted his own blood in his mouth. His head started spinning again.

Babulalji, Neil and Naseem Bhai were startled. They were not used to seeing Robin lose a fight. Neil began to cry.

"You are way out of your depth here, Robin. Stay down. But I have heard so much about you that I expected a little better from you in combat," Buru said.

Robin got up with some difficulty and said, "I can understand you being after the treasure and even killing people for it, Buru, but I don't understand why a historian and archaeologist like Dr. Verghese is involved in this?"

Buru smiled and said, "Dr. Verghese is an old business partner of mine, Robin. He is a historian by day and a smuggler of antiques by night. We have been running this business since a long time together. It's a deadly combination, you know! Being a historian and an archaeologist, he has information, knowledge and access to many antique idols and artifacts. He has even found many of them himself in archaeological excavations in India. And we have cleverly replaced many of the original idols and artifacts with the fake ones and sold them in various foreign markets."

Dr. Verghese interrupted, "Besides, what does one ever get through excavations and writing books about history and archaeology? A 'shawl' by the government as an appreciation of your work and a few lakh rupees? Or may be a mention in a small article about you on page three or four of a newspaper? These depress me. This business partnership with Buru has given me everything, I desired."

"But how did you come to know about the treasure of Raja Medini Ray?" Robin asked.

Dr. Verghese laughed and said, "It fell into my lap by itself! Professor Anand was a remarkable man. He had worked very hard on the history of Palamu. He had followed legends and rumours too and analysed them. He found out about the possible existence of an incredible treasure hidden in Palamu. But he was stuck with incomplete data and he needed help. He contacted me because of my reputation as an ace historian and archaeologist. I studied his work and found it to be correct. We together found the riddle and the coins in the underground tunnels of the Shahpur Fort, as I told you earlier also."

"But why did you get him killed?" Robin asked.

Buru laughed and said, "Did we? A ghost killed him! You saw the ghost too. Didn't you?"

Dr. Verghese said, "He knows about our ghost, Buru. When we had visited the fort earlier today, he knew how the torches were lit by themselves."

Babulalji, Neil and Naseem Bhai were surprised. So, it was not a real ghost after all. Robin had been skeptical about the ghost from the beginning.

Buru looked at Robin and said, "He is really a

remarkable detective. He makes me almost want not to kill him."

Dr. Verghese continued, "Buru and I planned to find the treasure and keep most of it for ourselves and give the rest to the government. Nobody knows how big the treasure is, so we had decided to ferret the major part of the treasure away before disclosing the 'find' to the world. It would have killed two birds with one stone. I would have become internationally famous for finding a great lost treasure and we would have valuables and artifacts to sell in the foreign grey market, too. But Professor Anand proved the biggest hurdle in our plan. So, we roped in two of his colleagues, Professor Anil and Professor Enos Baa. Before contacting me, he was working with both of them on this quest. We promised them fortunes if they helped us in convincing Professor Anand to join hands with us."

"But there were two problems. We had been working on the riddle for a long time but couldn't solve it and second, due to this delay, Professor Anand was growing impatient. Perhaps he suspected my intentions, so he hid the riddle and the coins. He wanted to go to the government with the riddle and the ancient coins. It would have taken the search for the treasure completely out of our hands. Then, all these government agencies would have been involved. So, we decided to eliminate him and also we needed someone who could find and solve that puzzle," Dr. Verghese said.

He paused, then went on, "So we made a plan. There was an old folk-lore popular in Palamu about a soldier named Satyabhama who had cursed the treasure and had sworn to protect it even after his death. He fitted the description of the 'knight' in the riddle who protects the treasure. Our next step was to create illusions of hauntings in the Palamu Fort and spread these rumours among the local populace. Then we planned to get Professor Anand killed by our 'ghost'. We involved Professor Anil in this plan and told him we were doing it just to take the riddle and the coin from him. He didn't know we were going to kill him."

Everyone was taken aback at this elaborate plan of deception and senseless killings. Meanwhile, Dr. Verghese continued, "Killing the Professor with an illusion of a killer ghost solved both our problems. The Professor was eliminated and you were brought into the case by the police department which wouldn't have happened if it was an ordinary homicide. Buru trusted you to solve the riddle and lead us to the treasure!"

Robin asked, "But, why did you get Professor Enos Baa killed?"

"He was not of sound mind. We didn't trust him. He once tried to warn Professor Anand about my intentions. Perhaps, he was the reason Professor Anand began to doubt me in the first place. Besides, killing him made even the police department and news channels believe that there was indeed a killer ghost in the city who was fulfilling his curse! He had two out of the five ancient coins with him. We took them after killing him and made it look like the ghost of Satyabhama had killed him to retrieve the coins," Dr. Verghese said to Robin.

Then, he went on with the gory story. "Imagine, Robin,

finding a treasure associated with so many mysteries and secrets would make one a national hero, wouldn't it? That is why we were passing the details of all these 'mysterious' happenings in anonymous, sealed envelopes to news channels so that we could spread this ghost story all over the state," Dr. Verghese said.

"And the attack on Professor Anil?" Robin asked.

Dr. Verghese said, "He was perturbed after we got Professor Anand killed. And when he saw that you had been brought in on this case, he got extremely nervous. He called me. I tried to calm him down and said I would come to Ranchi soon to explain everything to him. We knew you were suspecting his involvement in this conspiracy and were keeping him under surveillance. So, we staged an attack on him by the ghost and made sure that the constable assigned for his surveillance saw the attack happening and thought he had saved him. We were not very sure that it would make you believe that Professor Anil was not involved in the conspiracy, but we tried."

Buru interrupted, "We didn't know you had already worked out how we created the illusion of the haunting, otherwise we wouldn't have wasted our time on staging that attack. But hats off to you for working it out. We thought it was a brilliant idea and even you wouldn't be able to figure out how we did it."

"Yes, it was a brilliant idea, but the smell of garlic gave it away," Robin said.

"We clearly underestimated him, Buru," Dr. Verghese said.

He continued, "When we saw you had brilliantly found out the riddle and the coins from Professor Anand's house, I decided it was the right time to come to Ranchi. Buru's men were keeping an eye on your activities and we knew you were coming to Palamu. So, I reached here first and waited for you. Everything was going according to plan. But I am still not sure how you suspected me."

Robin replied, "When we visited Professor Anil's house, I saw an airline baggage sticker on his suitcase that indicated he had travelled recently from Thiruvananthapuram to Ranchi. And when I saw you, a historian from Kerala involved in this quest, I figured it can't be a coincidence. Probably Professor Anil knew you and had visited you there. That meant you were involved in this conspiracy, somehow. And when I told you that I had solved the riddle, in your excitement, you mentioned that 'they' were right. That meant someone had told you that I would solve the riddle. You were clearly working with someone else."

Dr. Verghese and Buru looked at each other and shrugged.

Buru took his gun out again and said, "Now Robin, we come back to the original question. Where is the treasure hidden in the fort?"

Robin looked at Babulalji, Neil and Tulsi. They were frightened. But Naseem Bhai was not. He was looking towards the top of the walls of the fort and the gate. Then he saw it. There was something shining on the top of the front wall. A small piece of glass, perhaps. He looked at Robin. Robin was looking straight at him.

Naseem Bhai winked at him. Robin looked at Buru and replied, "I don't know where the treasure is hidden. I just said I knew because I wanted to know what Dr. Verghese was up to."

Buru and Dr. Verghese were appalled.

"What? Is this a new game you are playing?" Dr. Verghese shouted.

Buru asked his men to bring Neil forward and pointed his gun at him. He said, "Let's see Robin how much you love your little cousin brother. Now tell me, where is the treasure hidden?"

Robin looked at him with eyes red with anger and said, "I told you not to point the gun at my friends."

Just then, a bullet was fired from the top of the Fort's wall that shattered the pistol Buru was carrying!

Robin jumped over Buru immediately and pinned him down on the ground. Multiple shots were fired from the wall of the fort and Buru's men who were holding Babulalji, Neil, Tulsi and Naseem Bhai were brought to the ground. Naseem Bhai pushed Babulalji and Neil inside the old mosque away from the range of the gunfire and dragged Tulsi inside too.

Buru's men retaliated with firepower, but the people who were shooting from above the walls were at a vantage position. Neil saw Dr. Verghese running towards the gate of the fort in a bid to escape. But as soon as he reached the gate, a villager in white *dhoti-kurta* with a gun in his hand, captured him and took him away. He looked towards the wall of the fort from where the shot had come that saved his life. Another local lad in white *dhoti-kurta* was there, too, shooting at Buru's men.

'What is happening? Why are the villagers helping us?' he thought.

Buru was furious. His whole plan was ruined.

"Detective Horo! You will pay for this!" he shouted.

"Oh no, he'll kill Horo Babu with his bare hands. Horo Babu is no match for him," Babulalji said to Neil looking at them from inside the mosque.

Buru attacked Robin once again with a right hook. Robin blocked it and planted a thunderous punch on his chest. Buru was thrown up a few feet. His head was spinning. It felt as if he had been hit by an iron hammer.

Babulalji and Neil were delighted!

Buru once again stood up and charged towards Robin who just stepped aside and Buru fell ahead because of his own momentum. When he turned back, Robin jumped and planted a ruthless round kick on his face. Blood gushed out of his mouth along with two of his teeth and he fell on the ground.

Buru was surprised. He had beaten Robin with just two blows a few minutes ago. But his mind was slowly drifting into darkness.

Robin went near him and lifted him by his collar.

"H…how did you…?" Buru asked.

"Are you referring to when you beat me with only two blows? I was just playing with your ego and was stalling you till the cavalry arrived. Here is another one for not listening when I told you specifically not to point a gun at my friends!" And with that, Robin planted a brutal punch on his nose.

Buru lost consciousness and fell to the ground.

Buru's men too were losing the gunfight. Most of them were either shot or severely injured. The remaining tried to flee and entered deep into the fort to find a way to escape from the ruins. But they were met by the special forces in the jungle. Most of them were captured but a few were able to flee.

Robin raised his hands towards the top of the wall. The villager with the gun responded.

Babulalji, Neil, Tulsi and Naseem Bhai came out of the old mosque. Neil hugged him.

"I knew you could beat that monster Buru easily. I never doubted you," Babulalji said happily.

Robin smiled.

He looked at Naseem Bhai and said, "Nice work, Naseem Bhai."

"Always there for you, Robin," Naseem Bhai replied with a smile.

Neil and Babulalji looked confused. Neil asked, "What just happened, Dada? Who are these villagers? Why were they helping us?"

Robin chuckled, "Oh! the villagers? Come, you should meet the 'nice' villagers! They are coming."

Two of the villagers clad in white *dhoti-kurta* were coming towards them. They were carrying guns.

One of the villagers was wearing a pair of black Aviator glasses!

"Inspector Patrick Minj!" Babulalji exclaimed.

"And Sub-inspector Collin Joseph," Robin said.

"Oh my God! It was them?" Neil was surprised and delighted at the same time.

Both of them had now reached the mosque where they were standing.

Inspector Patrick smiled and asked Neil, "So how was my shot that shattered Buru's gun?"

"Wicked!" Neil laughed and hugged him.

"What's with the boy? Is he my fan?" Inspector Patrick chuckled.

"Oh! The biggest!" Neil replied with a smile.

"Where is Dr. Verghese?" Robin asked.

"Sub-inspector Collin caught him when he was trying to escape. He is with us, don't worry," Inspector Patrick replied.

"Dada, I have no idea what happened here. How did Patrick Dada land up here with his men and the Special Forces?" Neil asked.

"Didn't you recognize me? I waved at your caravan

when you were crossing Kuru," Inspector Patrick told Neil.

"Oh my God! That was you?" Neil exclaimed in surprise.

Robin said, "I will explain everything, Neil. But the work is not completed here."

The Special Forces and Inspector Patrick's men had rounded up all of Buru's gang members. Ambulances were called for those who were injured. They also alerted the Forest Department to collect the carcass of the tiger.

They brought Dr. Verghese and Buru, who had regained consciousness, to where Robin was standing with Inspector Patrick and the others.

"You win this time, Robin," Buru said looking at Robin.

Robin looked at him but didn't say anything.

Dr. Verghese said in a desperate voice, "I don't think you lied, Robin. I know you have found the location of the treasure. Haven't you?"

All eyes were on Robin. Was he lying? Did he really know where the treasure was hidden?

"Do you really know, Horo Babu?" Babulalji asked.

Robin smiled and said,

"Yes, I do."

Chapter 42

Everyone was surprised.

"You really know where the treasure is hidden, Robin?" Inspector Patrick asked. Robin nodded in the affirmative.

"Where is it, Detective? Where is the last resting place of Satyabhama?" Dr. Verghese asked.

Robin thought for a second and said, "We were stuck on the last four lines of the riddle:

'The knight who quenches the thirst of the second,
The one who holds the water of stream,
For years to come till the end of time,
The Elixir of Doisa is protected by him'

As we have earlier determined that the 'two friends' in the riddle are none other than the two Palamu Forts, it is obvious that the 'second' here is the new fort which was built after the old fort. That means, the fort where we are standing right now harbours the unimaginable treasure. But where inside the new fort exactly?"

Everybody was listening to Robin without blinking their eyes.

Robin continued, "Doesn't it seem a bit odd that Raja Medini Ray got the very beautiful and fabled Nagpuri Gate bricked up? The very gate that he had imported at great expense? How many examples do we have in history that the gate of a fort was closed because it proved to be unlucky? I think none."

He continued, "The reason as we know it today was that the side on which the gate opened was unlucky, but don't you think the King must have consulted his Vaastu experts before installing that enormous gate? I think it was done purposefully, and not because it was unlucky. It was done to hide something."

"What do you mean, Horo Babu?" Babulalji asked. His eyes were wide open.

"Let's take a walk in the fort, Babulalji," Robin said and asked them to follow him.

He led the way and they followed him — as if he was the Pied Piper of Hamelin.

Robin stopped in front of a ruined structure inside the fort. It was damaged, but must have looked wonderful in its time.

"Do you know what it is, Tulsi?" Robin asked.

"Yes, Robin Bhaiyya. This used to be the *Rani Mahal.*

The Queen used to live here. The bedroom of the King and Queen was here too," Tulsi replied.

Robin nodded and said, "Exactly. But it was something more. It is documented in history that the greater part of this palace was used for one more thing. It was used to keep the treasure of the kingdom! It was the Queen's palace, so very few people had access to it and it was guarded heavily at all times by elite forces. The King used it as a treasury. It is clear that the Treasure of Doisa was kept here too initially. But we know it was later hidden by the King at some secret place. He needed to move the treasure away from here."

Robin stopped to think, then added, "But don't you think a treasure so massive would attract a lot of attention if moved outside? Where would you want to hide it? Someplace close I think, where it would be seen only by a handful of trusted people while it was being moved."

He pointed towards a tunnel situated a few meters from the '*Rani Mahal*' and continued, "I think this underground tunnel was used to transport the treasure into the safe custody of the 'Knight' who would protect it for years to come till the end of time!"

Dr. Verghese asked in excitement, "You mean the body of Satyabhama was buried where this tunnel finally opened?"

Robin looked at him and said, "I never said the 'knight' in the riddle was Satyabhama."

Chapter 43

“What?” everybody exclaimed.

“You mean the knight who is protecting the treasure is not Satyabhama? Then who is it?” Inspector Patrick asked.

“Don’t worry, I’ll take you to that knight. You don’t have to enter this tunnel to reach where he is. I know where this tunnel opens,” Robin said and asked them to follow him again.

Robin walked towards the courtyard of the fort again. He sat on the small stone wall around the water well in the courtyard.

He continued, “The man who wrote the riddle was never talking about Satyabhama in the last four lines of the riddle. He was talking about someone who ‘quenched the thirst’ of the second Fort of Palamu. The one who ‘held the water of the stream’. And who was it who held the water of the stream of the river *Ornaga* or *Auranga*? Who provided the water to quench the thirst of the people living in this fort?” he asked.

"You…you mean…" Buru could not complete his sentence.

Robin interrupted him, "Yes…I mean this water well! This 'water well' on which I am sitting is the 'Knight' that is protecting the treasure of 'Doisa'. The unimaginably vast and rich treasure of Raja Medini Ray is hidden deep inside this water well!"

They were dumbstruck by this revelation! It made perfect sense. The riddle did speak about someone who contained and provided water to the people of the second fort. It was the 'water well' in the courtyard of the new fort! The water it contained came from the *Ornaga* River.

Robin had solved the mysterious puzzle that had waited three hundred and fifty years in the womb of time for someone to come by and solve it. The puzzle that had been made up by Commander Trishul Singh centuries ago, was finally solved!

Robin continued, "The underground tunnel that we saw near the *Rani Mahal* leads to this well. In olden times, the Queen used to walk through that tunnel to reach the water well for bathing. It was, therefore, very convenient for Raja Medini Ray to transport the large treasure through that tunnel situated near the treasury and hide it inside this well. It was always guarded by his elite forces. This well used to be much deeper in those times. I am sure if one digs it deep enough, one will find some secret vault that safeguarded the treasure from the eyes of enemies for centuries!"

Everyone was amazed and speechless. They were not

able to absorb the feeling that deep beneath their feet lay the treasure of the greatest King of Palamu.

Robin stood up from the stone wall of the water well and looked inside it.

"One could never suspect that this old and neglected water well was protecting the magnificent treasure for more than three hundred and fifty years like a silent 'knight'." said Robin.

Then he turned towards Inspector Patrick and said, "Inspector Patrick, I have given you the killers of Professor Anand and Professor Enos Baa. And the treasure of the greatest King of Palamu, Raja Medini Ray, too. You need to inform the Government of Jharkhand about this so that they can get it assessed by the department concerned. I think my work here is done."

Inspector Patrick shook his hand and said, "I can't thank you enough, Robin. Even I had lost all hope of solving this mystery. I even doubted you sometimes. But I am grateful that in spite of all odds, you have solved this mystery. I still have so many questions to ask you, but let's get home first and get these criminals put behind bars. Then I'll take you all out for a treat and we will discuss this at leisure."

Robin smiled and said, "Yes guys, let's go home."

They all left the Palamu Fort. The Special Forces helped Inspector Patrick and his men to move Dr. Verghese, Buru and the criminals of his gang to Ranchi.

Robin, Babulalji, Neil, Tulsi and Naseem Bhai went

towards their caravan. Naseem Bhai looked proudly at the mark of the tiger's claw on his caravan, but they all were sad for him because he had been killed by Buru's gang members.

It was evening by the time they reached Amwa village where they had to drop Tulsi. They thought of meeting Guni Mahto before leaving Palamu. When they reached his house, his grandson Kamal informed them about his sudden death.

"When you left today morning, he sat outside his hut for a long time. Then he gave this coin to me and asked me to give it to you when you came back and went to sleep inside his hut. When I went to wake him up for tea, he was already dead," Kamal said, handing over the gold coin with the picture of Raja Medini Ray embossed on it to Robin.

Robin was sad. He looked at the coin in his hand and remembered the old man fondly. Probably, the last man who knew about the legend of Satyabhama and his beloved King had died, but not before passing on their magnificent story to them. Some stories are never meant to die.

They stayed in Amwa village to attend the last rites of Guni Mahto, while Inspector Patrick headed to Ranchi with the Special Forces.

The next morning after attending the last rites ceremony, they thanked Tulsi and took their leave. They invited Tulsi to visit them in Ranchi sometimes. Then, they finally left Palamu.

They reached home at around 5:00 pm. Somra was eagerly waiting for them. He opened the gate and Naseem

Bhai drove the caravan inside.

Neil and Babulalji told Somra all about their adventures in Palamu. He was delighted and thrilled.

They all wanted to ask so many questions to Robin about how the crooks had managed to make the illusion of the ghost so real and how had Inspector Patrick reached the fort. But Robin said he would disclose everything only when Inspector Patrick took them out for their promised treat.

In the prime time news of Channel News 11 that night, Atreyi Biswas was running another story, 'Exorcism of the Ghost of Palamu Fort by Detective Horo.'

Robin smiled.

They slept well that night, for they knew the morning would bring answers to some of the questions that still remained.

Chapter 44

In the morning, they all woke up early. They were ready waiting for Inspector Patrick in the garden of Robin's house. Robin was reading the newspaper. The front page was splashed with the news of the ghost, the secret of the mysterious murders and the finding of the location of the treasure in the Palamu Fort by Detective Horo.

There was news of Professor Anil and Bheem being involved in the murder of Professor Anand, and of their arrest too.

They heard the familiar sound of the horn of Inspector Patrick's jeep. Neil ran and opened the gate. Inspector Patrick was in a white polo T- shirt and navy-blue jeans.

"So where are we going for the treat?" he asked.

"It's been a long time since we ate *Litti-chokha* near the Ranchi High Court. Can we go there?" Neil asked.

They all agreed, readily.

A few minutes later, they were sitting at a *Litti-chokha* shop near the High Court and were enjoying their food.

"So, Robin now you have to answer some questions," Inspector Patrick said, taking a bite of *litti* dipped in ghee.

"Yes, of course, I'll clear every doubt. Ask," Robin said.

"Horo Babu, first of all, tell us how the illusion of the ghost was created?" Babulalji asked.

Robin looked at him and replied, "It was a brilliant idea. At first, even I was not sure how it was done. But the smell of garlic with the white smoke was making me uneasy. It felt there was something I was missing. I believed that it was some conspiracy, right from the beginning, but I was not quite sure how it was being done. But on the night when the ghost of Satyabhama came to our house and our curtains caught fire spontaneously, it dawned on me how it was being done, especially when I saw a matchstick in between Naseem Bhai's lips."

"A matchstick? Of course, we all know a matchstick is used to light a fire. But how does it explain the magical fire that would spring up when the ghost used to arrive?" Inspector Patrick asked.

"No, there is more to it than a simple matchstick. When I saw the matchstick between Naseem Bhai's lips, I remembered that its tip is of red phosphorus. When I remembered this, I recalled one more fact — that there is white phosphorous also which burns spontaneously when exposed to air. That is why it is always stored under water," explained Robin.

He continued, "Guess what? When it burns, it produces a 'white smoke', a reddish-coloured residue and a very typical smell. Any guesses what that smell is?"

"Smell of garlic?" Neil guessed.

"Bingo! It produces a smell that resembles the smell of garlic!" Robin replied with a smile.

"It is also used by armies to produce smoke grenades, smoke screens and various bombs. It was clear they were using white phosphorus to create their illusionary ghost. But the question was how?" Robin continued.

Babulalji asked, "Yes, Horo Babu, how did the curtains catch fire?"

Robin replied, "They used different techniques every time. In Professor Anand's house, we had found a sandstone tumbler with a hole at its bottom. The hole was made intentionally. Professor Anil must have filled the tumbler with water and placed a piece of white phosphorus inside it. He had kept the hole closed initially and when he planted it near the table at Professor Anand's study, he must have opened the hole and kept a corner of the curtain inside it. The curtain was sprayed with some odourless oil or fuel, obviously by Bheem, beforehand. He must have done it when the Professor went down to meet his visitors, Dilip and Syril. The water slowly dripped out of the tumbler as Professor Anil sat with Professor Anand in his library. They had timed it perfectly with the appearance of the 'ghost' who was obviously a member of Buru's gang. The water in the tumbler dripped out slowly till finally the white phosphorus was exposed to air. It caught fire spontaneously and burnt the curtains with it, producing white smoke and the characteristic smell of garlic! They must have planted more such tumblers inside the room to produce more smoke and in their hurry to flee, they must have forgotten to remove the one that was behind the table."

There was more to explain, so Robin continued, "The same technique was used in creating the haunting at the Palamu Fort. They had kept pieces of white phosphorous under water inside the iron-torches fixed on the walls of the passageway with a very small hole at the bottom which allowed the water to drip out slowly exposing the white phosphorous to the air which caught fire spontaneously and burned the flammable material inside the torches."

They were listening intently to all that Robin had to say.

Inspector Patrick asked, "What about the curtains at Professor Enos Baa's house? They caught fire spontaneously, too, in front of us. There were no tumblers there."

Robin replied, "Probably, a different technique was used there. White phosphorus dissolves readily in hydrogen sulphide solution and remains inert inside it. But when this solution with white phosphorus inside is kept in the open air, the hydrogen sulphide slowly evaporates in the air leaving behind the exposed white phosphorus which again catches fire spontaneously! And that is what they did in Professor Enos Baa's house. They had sprayed the curtains with hydrogen sulphide solution containing dissolved white phosphorous. The hydrogen sulphide was evaporating slowly and when it did so completely, the exposed white phosphorus caught fire spontaneously burning the curtain with it and producing a white smoke and the smell of garlic."

He then attempted to explain what had happened in his own house. "The same technique was used in our house, too, where a member of Buru's gang must have sprayed the same solution on our curtains while another member disguised as Satyabhama appeared in front of us to make us believe in the ghost story."

Neil asked, "But Dada, how did the copy of the riddle that Professor Anil had made on paper burned spontaneously?"

Robin replied, "The same solution of hydrogen sulphide and white phosphorous was used, Neil. He had sprayed the solution on that paper too and had kept it on the table. The paper caught fire when the chemical evaporated completely, producing the white smoke."

"My God! We were taken for a ride and we believed it!" Neil said.

"There is no need to feel ashamed, Neil. Initially, even I didn't understand how they did it. It was a simple trick but when it was played in front of our eyes with the story they had woven around it, it felt real," Robin replied.

Babulalji thought about something for a few minutes, then asked, "Horo Babu, when the ghost had attacked Professor Anil, the constable had seen it. He said the ghost appeared out of smoke and then disappeared inside it. How did that happen?"

"In Professor Anil's house, a smoke screen was created by exposing the phosphorous in the air and a pre-recorded video of the ghost was projected on the smokescreen with the help of a projector. Bheem removed it when the constable tried to enter the house. That's why it must have taken him some time to open the door, and he made up a story that he had been sleeping," Robin replied.

"What about the blueish-coloured fire on the arms of the ghost?" Babulalji asked again.

Robin had an answer for that as well. "You are carrying it in your bag too, Babulalji!"

"In my bag? What?" Babulalji asked in surprise.

"Yes, you do carry a hand sanitizer in your bag, don't you?" Robin asked.

"Yes, I do, but what of that?" Babulalji asked.

Robin asked him to take it out and spilled it on the bench. Then he took a matchbox from the shop and ignited it. It burned with a blueish hue. Robin lifted the burning hand sanitizer on his fingers too.

He said, "See! It burns with a blueish flame and does not produce much heat either. They must have used some similar compound with protective padding on the arms."

Babulalji asked in surprise, "Horo Babu, how do you know all these things? Do you burn everything to check its colour?"

Robin smiled.

"But Dada, how did Patrick Dada reach Palamu Fort with the Special Forces?" Neil asked.

Robin looked at Naseem Bhai and said with a smile, "I knew Buru's men were tracking our movements. I saw one of them near the office of Channel News 11, too. Initially, I was not sure why they were creating this illusion of the ghost repeatedly and risking getting caught. But when I found the riddle in Professor Anand's house, I realized it was done to bring me on the case so that I solve the riddle and lead them to the treasure. That was why they were following us everywhere."

Robin continued, "I knew they would tail us to Palamu Fort, too. That's why me and Naseem Bhai decided to ask Inspector Patrick to follow us, disguised as simple village folks. Inspector Patrick also took permission from the IG of Police for taking help of the Special Forces if needed. Naseem Bhai was constantly in contact with Inspector Patrick. I asked him to be in contact because I thought Buru's men would concentrate mostly on my activities and probably pay very little attention to him. When we stayed at Tulsi's house in Amwa village, Inspector Patrick had come near the house at night to ask about the next day's plan. Naseem Bhai met him at night and conveyed to him our plans for the next day. He also told him about our suspicions about Dr. Verghese, too."

Robin paused for a moment and then continued, "When we reached the *dhaba* while returning from the fort, the first time, and saw Buru's men there, I asked Naseem Bhai to inform Inspector Patrick about it. He did it before we were caught by the gang.

In the fort also, when Buru pointed the gun at Neil, I looked at Naseem Bhai to ask if Inspector Patrick had arrived. He saw him on the wall of the fort and signalled to me with a wink. And then I gave Buru a nice beating when Inspector Patrick had shattered his gun with a magnificent gunshot and thereby released Neil whom he had taken as hostage."

"I think all the loose ends are tied now. Any more questions?" Robin asked again.

Naseem Bhai asked, "Robin, there is a question of daggers of Satyabhama which were used to kill Professor Anand and Enos Baa. They were examined by experts and they said they were actually antiques belonging to some old dynasty. Where did they get hold of Satyabhama's daggers?"

Robin replied, "Dr. Verghese and Buru were smugglers of antiques, Naseem Bhai. It was very easy for them to find some old antique daggers. These were completely some random antique daggers which they projected as the daggers of Satyabhama, because how could anybody know whether Satyabhama actually carried daggers or not? Besides, we don't even know whether a person named Satyabhama actually existed in the Kingdom of Palamu or not. He is not documented in history. Everything we know about him is from a story a good old man told us.... And that is the beauty of a story...

It could be true, or it could be false...."

EPILOGUE

ONE MONTH LATER

Somra was woken up by the horn of a vehicle outside the gate. He looked at the wall clock. It was 6:30 am. He took out the keys and opened the door and then went towards the gate. He felt the cool morning breeze as he walked to the gate. He peeped through the hole of the gate and saw Inspector Patrick standing outside with his jeep.

'What is he doing here so early in the morning? Is everything all right?' he asked himself before hurriedly opening the gate.

"Is Robin still sleeping?" Inspector Patrick asked while entering the gate.

"Yes, he is still sleeping. Come in, I'll wake him up. Is everything all right?" Somra asked.

"Never better, Somra. Go and wake him up. It's very important," Inspector Patrick said with a smile. "Where are Neil and Babulalji?" he continued.

Somra replied, "Babulalji left around two weeks back

and Neil went home yesterday. His holidays were over."

"He missed it just by one day! Anyways, he'll get to know. Everybody will know," Inspector Patrick said.

Somra went up and woke Robin up.

"So he came. I was expecting him today, but not this early in the morning," Robin said and asked Somra for tea for both of them. He wrapped a light green-coloured shawl around him and came down.

Inspector Patrick was sitting in the Drawing room with a newspaper in his hands. He saw Robin and said in excitement, "Do you know what happened yesterday evening, Robin?"

Robin came and sat next to the Inspector on the sofa and said, "Our Government finally found the treasure of Raja Medini Ray inside the old water well at the Palamu Fort."

Inspector Patrick was taken aback. "Do you really have some super powers? How did you know?" he asked.

Robin smiled and said, "No, I don't have any superpowers. The Honourable Chief Minister of Jharkhand himself called me yesterday night to tell me about it and thanked me for solving the riddle."

"Oh, did he? We were called in for an emergency meeting yesterday evening at the Honourable Chief Minister's residence. We were informed that our Government Agencies including the Archaeological Survey of India were working on the excavations at the Palamu Fort. Yesterday morning, they uncovered an enormous vault deep beneath the very water well Detective Horo had asked us to look in. And when they opened the vault, they found the great treasure of the Chero Dynasty inside it!

He said it was a glorious day in the history of Jharkhand as we would be able to know more about our history and the world will know how rich our heritage is. He said the treasure and the artifacts found in the excavation are of great historical importance. Experts are saying that the treasure is so enormous that it would take them months to determine the actual value of it.

It is indeed the greatest find of the century, Robin. And it all became possible because of you."

Robin smiled and said, "It was team effort, Inspector Patrick."

"Yes, it was. And talking about the team, I am telling this to you unofficially, but yesterday it was planned in the meeting that you, me, Babulalji, Neil and Naseem Bhai would be invited to the Honourable CM's house for a special lunch and a press conference where we will be felicitated," Inspector Patrick said.

He continued, "By the way, Syril got bail from the lower court itself and Professor Anil and Bheem have agreed to testify against Dr. Verghese and Buru. Now, I think this case has reached its closure."

Robin came out with Inspector Patrick to see him off. He left in his jeep. Robin looked up to the sky.

An orange sun was rising in the distant horizon. He sat in the garden wrapped in his light green-coloured shawl holding a cup of hot steaming tea in his hand and thought:

'No matter how dark the night is, it cannot ever keep the sun from rising.'

Acknowledgment

- A very special thanks to the ETERNITY BAND for making the Original Soundtrack "KOHRA" for The secret of the Palamu Fort.

  ETERNITY is a Progressive indie rock and Doom metal band from Jamshedpur, Jharkhand, with amazing Vocals and Lyrics by Kunal, with lead Guitarist Vishal, Bass by Himanshu and Drums by Anand.

  (http://www.facebook.com/Eternityband4/)

  (https://www.instagram.com/eternitybandjsr)

- Bibhu Datta Rout for putting in lots of time and effort for the book despite being terribly busy. He is one of the most important reasons this book became possible.
- Pratishtha Gupta, Divya Mirchandani, Reena Singh, Prashant Gurav and Hitesh Jain from StoryMirror for everything they did for the book.
- Mr. Kundan Kumar Choudhary, Feature editor, Jharkhand, Dainik Bhaskar, for providing valuable inputs and suggestions for the book.
- Mrs.Atreyi Biswas Roy for her inputs and suggestions.

- Dr. Vijay Kumar Mishra, Dr. Sanjay Kumar and Dr. Patrick Prabodh Minj for their support throughout the project.
- Dr. Ajay Kumar Singh, Dr. Manjula Sinha, Dr. Rajesh Singh, Dr. Souvik Choudhury, Dr. Atri Gangopadhyay and Dr. Praveen Upadhyay for their valuable inputs and suggestions.
- Mr. Sanjay Bose and Mr. Chandrika from the Third Eye Digital Studio, Ranchi and Mr Ayush for their immense contribution in making the video of 'Kohra'.